The White Bicycle

The White Bicycle

Beverley Brenna

Red Deer Press

5 4 3

Published by Red Deer Press
195 Allstate Parkway, Markham
ON, L3R 4T8
www.reddeerpress.com

Edited for the Press by Peter Carver
Cover image courtesy of Taylor Crowe
Cover design by Daniel Choi

We acknowledge with thanks the Canada Council for the Arts, and the Ontario Arts Council for their support of our publishing program. We acknowledge the financial support of the Government of Canada through the Canada Book Fund (CBF) for our publishing activities.

Canada Council for the Arts
Conseil des Arts du Canada

ONTARIO ARTS COUNCIL
CONSEIL DES ARTS DE L'ONTARIO

Library and Archives Canada Cataloguing in Publication
Brenna, Beverley A
White bicycle / Beverley Brenna.
ISBN 978-0-88995-483-0
1. Asperger's syndrome--Juvenile fiction. I. Title.
PS8553.R382W45 2012 jC813'.54 C2012-905183-7

Publisher Cataloging-in-Publication Data (U.S.)
Brenna, Beverley.
White bicycle / Beverley Brenna.
[208] p. : cm.
Summary: A young woman with Asperger's Syndrome travels to the south of France with her mother and friends and strives for independence. This is a story about life, obstacles and ultimately, the dignity found in the search for independence.
ISBN: 978-0-88995-483-0 (paper)
1. Asperger's syndrome – Juvenile fiction. 2. Autonomy in adolescence – Juvenile fiction. I. Title.
[Fic] dc23 PZ7.B7466Wh 2012

Printed in Canada

MIX
Paper from responsible sources
FSC® C016245

For my grandmother,
Jane Taylor (Jeannie) Martin Stilborn

Lourmarin, France
Monday, August 4, 2003

My Dream

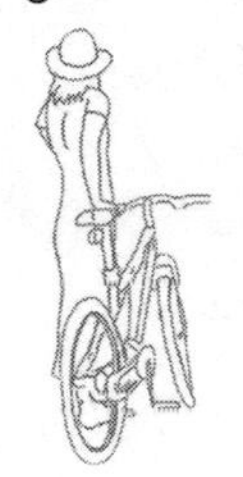

In my dream, I am stumbling along a difficult path in the woods. Tree roots and rocks are underfoot, and vines catch at my ankles. It is very hot, and the silvery olive trees provide little shade. I can hear my mother hollering, "Taylor Jane! Come back!", but I do not obey her, because it is embarrassing to be called after when you are nineteen years old. In my arms I carry a white bicycle, which I cannot put down. It is heavy and I am tired, but I keep walking. At last the path becomes a road, and I ride. The speed and the wind on my face are exhilarating. I forget about my mother; I forget how difficult the white bicycle is to carry; I forget about everything except the journey ahead.

I do not know whether this is really a dream or a nightmare. My mother would say it is a nightmare because it has unhappy parts in it; but so does life, and life is closer to dreams than nightmares. In life it is your dreams that take you forward, and your dreams that make you human. This is something I have been thinking about a lot lately.

I am sitting in my bedroom overlooking the cherry orchard, and the white bicycle is leaning up against the trunk of a tree. I am planning to ride it later, but I will probably stay on the road. I remember all too well what happens when I take the white bicycle into the forest.

Other Dreams

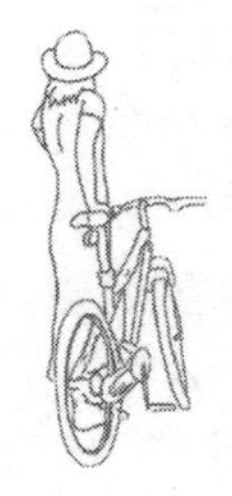

The word "dream" carries many meanings, and I am thinking about two other types of dreams I have in addition to the sleeping dream about the white bicycle.

1. I dream of adding pieces to my life story, pieces that were not included in my previous journals. There is much about my life as a child that I want to revisit through writing, and much about that life I do not ever, ever want to forget. While those times were difficult, they are part of who I am now, and should not be passed over in a story of my life. And maybe the past will help me to better understand the present. My high-school history teacher used to say that the past is important to the present. I will explore my past, such as it is, and see if this is true.

2. I dream of a future where I am independent, able to work and take care of myself. It is possible that my writing will help me achieve this goal. My high-school English

teacher said that sometimes writing stuff down makes you feel better. I have translated this to mean that writing words about my life helps me to understand better the situations I am describing. If I do not understand something when it happens to me, I can work on it as one might work on a puzzle, through my writing, piece by piece.

I should have begun this journal a long time ago, because we have already been in France a whole month, but I have been busy getting used to my new schedule. I have to get up at 7 AM in order to help Martin Phoenix eat his breakfast, as that is part of my job as a babysitter. Martin Phoenix is really too old to have a babysitter—he will be in grade eight next fall—but because he has personal care needs related to his cerebral palsy, there has to be someone with him all the time. Maybe "personal care assistant" is a better match. I will speak to his father about this. Then I will put "personal care assistant" on my resumé.

"Personal care assistant" looks a lot better than "babysitter" on a resumé but either term could support further employment. That is my main goal: employment so I can buy all my own clothes, and everything else I will need. My mother has just now gone into town to see if she can find me something nicer to wear, but what I am wearing is a perfectly good jean dress. I do not know why she is not satisfied with it. I have begun to think that my mother is never satisfied with clothing once it is a year old. She could end up doing a lot of shopping with an attitude like that.

This story will be about how I got to France for two months of summer employment. But it starts long before this, in Saskatoon, Saskatchewan, Canada. What I have written in my other journals does not go back far enough, and does not present the set of first-person images I carry inside me: images of being a child, and going to school, and the bewilderment of understanding no one, and of being misunderstood. Those journals do not tell much about my father leaving home when I was eight and they certainly do not tell about all the yelling my parents did against each other. Things were uneasy for me most of the time in those days.

Until I learned about my diagnosis of Asperger's Syndrome when I was eleven, I had no explanation for why some things were so difficult for me. Why, for example, when people spoke too fast all I heard was vowel sounds. And why feelings suddenly exploded in my head until all I could see was white. It is possible my parents blamed each other for my challenges, thinking I had not been raised well, or that I was too much like one or the other of them in my stubbornness. But I don't think I broke their marriage in half. They were just getting in each other's way. My mother wanted to date men who wore polyester golf shirts and then progress to dating my friend Luke Phoenix's father, Alan Phoenix, who looks like the actor Kevin Costner. My father wanted to open a business in Cody, Wyoming and move there and get a girlfriend named Sadie Richards who looks like the actress Julia Roberts. Neither my mother nor my father could do these things as long as they were married together.

I remember being happy in the time period before I went to kindergarten, although my mother tells a different story. In my memory, before-school was a time when I did what I wanted, when I wanted, and there was very little opportunity for anger. In my mother's memory, before-school was just as bad as once-school-started. But mothers don't know everything, and in my case, mine actually knows very little. I don't know if she's lying when she talks about my early childhood, or if memories have escaped from a hole in her collection. Either way, she's wrong about the before-school period. I barely wore any clothes then, which was altogether pleasant; it wasn't until I was five that I had to bear any kind of scratchy cloth against my body when I didn't feel like it. Unfortunately, there was a rule that said you had to wear clothes to kindergarten. One of my earliest memories of school is sitting on a hard bench with my skin hurting all over from the clothes, and watching other kids climb and slide on an apparatus that looked very dangerous. Part of me wanted to climb up there as well, but the other part of me was afraid, and that is the part that won.

I am working hard not to let the "afraid" part win, now that I am nineteen years old. I do not want to be like Stanley in Harold Pinter's play, *The Birthday Party*, who never left his bedroom and who was at the mercy of his landlady. I am referring to Harold Pinter the playwright, not Harold Pinter my gerbil, who is in Canada with his son, Samuel Beckett, getting looked after by my friend Shauna. Technically, Harold Pinter the gerbil is a female, being Samuel Beckett's mother, but gender can be flexible and so I think of him as male, just as his name suggests.

I am working especially hard not to let the afraid part win each time I think about my future, although it reminds me of a precipice that if I am not careful I will just fall from. Instead of hiding in my bedroom, I am putting one foot in front of another—just like the old woman I met last week in Cassis. If she can do it, when she was probably about a hundred years old, then so can I. I hope she is not dead. My mother said we can find out by phoning the hospital, but I do not remember her name.

This journal is to investigate my thoughts and feelings, like my English teacher advised me to do. It is to take the steps I have collected in my journey so far—*en cachette,* the French would say—and privately explore them as best I can. It is also to write about the dreams that carry me forward. It is not to blame anyone for my misery, or my joy; it just tells it like it was.

There is a little gray book on the wooden bookshelf in my bedroom here in France that intrigues me. It is a discussion of consciousness, by Jean-Paul Sartre. Jean-Paul Sartre says that it is critical to select the order of our bits of knowledge, to set things out in a way that makes sense in our own personal search for freedom. That is what I am considering now as I sort through my memories and begin this journal. What to put first, what to put second, and where to place all the things that must somehow fit together to compose a person, to create a life. My life, such as it is.

I think I will start by writing about France, and how I got here, and the events that fill my time. Then I will go back and tell about my childhood. And then I will come forward and see if I have learned anything important.

The Butterflies in France

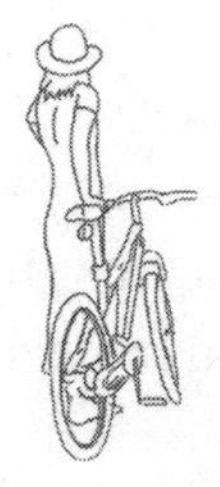

There are many different kinds of butterflies in France, but I have not seen any Painted Lady ones. The most common here in the south are the Swallowtail, the Large White, the Small White, the Pale Clouded Yellow, the Clouded Yellow, and the Wood White. We found a Wood White on the side of the car one day, and my mother said it was a moth, but I know she is wrong. My mother is often wrong and that is one reason I do not want to listen to her. For one thing, the Wood White butterfly's antennae had rounded clubs on the ends. For another, its wings were held vertically as it rested. It did have a fuzzy body, but so do some other butterflies that are not moths.

When I look for butterflies, I always make sure to find seven of them. Then I start a new search. I do not restrict my findings to one species, because that would be too difficult. Just seven butterflies, in total, and then I begin again. One day I did see seven Pale Clouded Yellow ones, though, and that was a good day indeed.

The old woman in Cassis was wearing a nightgown that had butterflies on it, and I wonder if she was thinking about flying when she headed toward the sea. I wish I could remember her name so that I could phone the hospitals. It sounded something like Kool-Aid, but it was not that. Maybe we will go sightseeing to Cassis again, and I can ask someone where the hospital is or find it on the map. Then I could go in and ask whether a woman wearing a butterfly nightgown was brought there, and what happened to her. When I pulled her out of the water, she did not look as if she was going to die. But then again, my grandmother died in the spring and she did not look as if she was going to die either. Nothing was sticking out of her, like you see in movies when people get shot or stabbed. All my grandmother had was pneumonia, which I have had twice—but it killed her. My mother said she was *only* 75, and I do not know what she meant by that. There isn't an age you can be in addition to being 75, is there? Either you're 75 or you're not, and my grandmother was.

Traveling to France

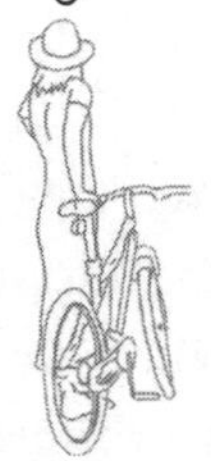

Making up your mind means making a decision. Once I made up my mind to go to France for the summer, I told my mother and she made up her own mind to come along. At first I did not particularly want her to come, but then I decided that it would be okay. She had the right amount of money from Grandma's will, and she said she had been waiting a long time to take a summer off and travel. Having my mother in France with me will not prevent me from putting the job with Martin Phoenix on my resumé, and that is the main thing I care about, although sometimes I regret letting her join us. She keeps trying to be the boss of me.

A few weeks before our trip to France, we drove to the airport in Saskatoon and watched the airplanes landing and lifting off. Then my mother took me to a parking lot near the edge of the city where we simulated an airplane on the runway. She brought out a hair dryer and an electric razor, plugged them into the double-socket cigarette-lighter-adapter she got at a garage sale, and turned them on. I put my hands over my ears and my mother offered me earplugs, but I didn't want them. Then my mother drove the car over bumpy potholes until my teeth banged together.

"Okay, enough!" I said. "This is not a smart way to spend our time." I turned off the hair dryer and the electric razor.

"You'll thank me when we take off in the airplane and it doesn't bother you," my mother said.

"It would make more sense for you to use the razor on your chin," I said. "You are growing a beard."

My mother felt her chin and began to laugh.

"Easy to say, but you'll be glad we practiced when you get into the airplane," she said. "And maybe I will shave my chin before we go to France. Or get a waxing, or whatever they do. Heck, maybe I'll get the whole works—a pedicure, a facial, everything. After all, it's *France*."

I do not know what she meant by that but getting the pedicure was a mistake. They accidentally cut into the base of her big toenail with one of their tools and the chemicals got in there and killed the nail. Now she has an ugly yellow crust for a toenail and she will have this ugly thing on her foot until the new toenail grows in. *If* it grows in. I prefer cutting my own fingernails and toenails and I will continue to do so; it is much smarter to take care of yourself than to have somebody else do it, especially if that person has sharp instruments and shaky hands. And chemicals.

We left for France on Friday, July 4. On the airplane my mother and I watched a movie, just like we used to do in the old days—except when we watched movies together at home we weren't on a plane. The movie was *Mary Poppins,* and we saw it on the tiny TV screens that hung on the back of the seats ahead of us. We had seen *Mary Poppins* together when I was little and it was interesting seeing it again because some parts I remembered and some parts I did not. I remembered all the things the children said, but nothing Mary Poppins said. This time, I found Mary Poppins the most interesting character because she was a governess. Governess is the old word for babysitter, and if I was living in the past I would be putting "governess" on my resumé for the summer.

If my mother had blue eyes, she would look like the actress Julie Andrews who plays Mary Poppins. My mother, however, cannot sing, although she sometimes tries hard. When I think about my mother and me on the plane, it is like I am watching a film, replaying the images as if they were happening right now. I can see her sitting there, leaning forward and laughing, as Mary Poppins slides up the banister.

"Don't sing along," I say to my mother when the music starts, but she will not listen and keeps singing very quietly. I am not overwhelmed by the experience of the airplane, as she had predicted I would be, but I am bothered by my mother.

On the airplane, I feel very restless and clean the tray in front of me seven times with a piece of damp paper towel. Then I walk up and down the aisle until the person in the blue jacket comes and tells me I need to sit down because of turbulence. I do not think I am rocking the plane but I suppose when you are up in the air, a bit of weight in the wrong place can make a difference.

When I sit down, I look at my mother and say, "You have a very smooth chin."

"Thank you," she says, and laughs. We have supper, which she eats and I do not because it is something disgusting rolled up in a pancake.

We land in Toronto, change planes, and then land in New York to change planes again. When we look at the digital signboard in the New York airport to find our departure gate, our flight is missing. I think we should go and find another signboard, but my mother says we have to talk to a ticket agent. Even though there is a long line of passengers waiting to speak to an agent, two of the agents are sitting on their stools visiting while one of the other agents is just working at her computer. I crane my neck to see what she is doing. Maybe she is playing a computer game because she is a computer game addict. After seventeen minutes, which I time on my atomic watch, we are called to a station where a man who looks like the father in Mary Poppins tells us about our trip delay.

Apparently because our plane was late landing in New York, we missed our connecting flight to Munich—which was then supposed to take us to Marseille, where Alan Phoenix is meeting us in a car. Because we missed our connection, we have to stay overnight here in New York and take another plane the next morning.

"See," I say. "When one thing changes, everything changes."

My mother gets the H of wrinkles in her forehead.

"Never mind about that now," she says.

Before we leave the airport, my mother wants to go to the washroom and makes me go with her to hold her purse. There is a digital sign above the sink that says when the washroom was last cleaned. I wish we had one of those signs at home. It would keep track of how clean things are and it could also help me remember not to clean something that is already clean. I believe I will put "digital sign" on my Christmas list.

After my mother uses the washroom, we stop at an airport café for supper and I watch the news on a big digital TV screen. New York is really a digital place. The news on the television is very confusing. There is a live-action broadcast where someone announces current events, but it is hard to hear. Simultaneously, there is a line of text at the bottom of the screen, with words that tell about different news stories. I read about a woman in Bangladesh whose husband beat her because she was getting an education. At the same time, I see a picture of a group of smiling children and a clown dancing around a big cake that is decorated with red, white, and blue stripes. These two stories do not go together. I have enough trouble keeping messages clear without having two opposite feeds coming in from the television.

I turn my body away from the TV and look at the people around me. There is a cute guy sitting at the next table. He is wearing blue jeans, and I think he might be a "ten." I would ask Shauna if she were here, but she is not. I wonder if her husband is a "ten."

"Everything is changing because one thing changed," I say again to Mom.

"Stop telling me that," Mom says. "You're making me crazy."

I am about to tell her that she can be crazy without my help, but there is a man at another table who is talking on his cell phone so loudly that I cannot concentrate.

"I'm sorry ... say that again," he yells. "Okay. Okay. Well, let me get her New Canaan number and I can phone her and leave a message with my email address. Yes, even if she isn't there right now, it will be fine to leave a message."

"You shouldn't give out your email address!" I say.

"Hush, Taylor," says my mother.

"Thanks a lot. You too," says the man, but I don't think he says it to me. He says it into the phone.

"Well, that's the rule," I say. "You never know who is going to be at the other end of the—"

"Hello? Hello! Before you hang up, I just need to ask one more—"

"I hope it's a safety question," I say to my mother. "If he does not know her phone number, he obviously does not know her well enough to share his email address."

"It's not your business," says my mother, standing up. "Come on, we should go and find our hotel."

As if it would be lost.

"How many stars does it have?" I ask. "What if we don't like it? Just because the airline paid for it, do we have to stay there?" I know that the better hotels have five stars, the average ones have four, and the duds have three or less.

"I'm sure it will be fine," says my mother and heads off so quickly that I have to run to catch up with her. This is what I hate about my mother. She does not always tell the truth. In fact, some people might call her a big fat liar, even though she is not very tall and not very wide, either.

Overnight in New York

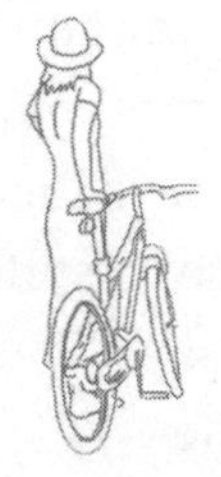

The hotel we are staying at is not in the airport. And instead of waiting for the shuttle, as the airport lady told us to do, my mother insists that we take a city bus. I am glad about this because I have never taken a shuttle before and I do not want to take one this day.

"I'm not waiting for an hour when the other bus comes right away," my mother says.

She is correct and the city bus does come right away. There are bus stops just before the intersections, not after them like in Saskatoon. The bus driver is careful and waits until the light turns green before he pulls out. Suddenly I see a man running after the bus, but he is not fast enough to catch up.

"Stop!" yells one of the other passengers. "There's a man wants to get on."

"Not allowed," says the bus driver. "I can only stop at the bus stops. Regulations."

"Hard-hearted," says someone from behind me.

"Look at that guy run!" says another.

"You'd think there'd be some flexibility here," says someone else.

We go on like this for another block, through a green light, and the man is still running. He must really want to be on this bus.

I look around at the scenery. There are warehouses and I think they look like buildings the Mafia would be in. I tell this to my mother and she tells me to stop worrying. But she looks out the window and I think she looks worried too. She has that H of wrinkles in the middle of her forehead.

"The Mafia have big cars with colored windows," I say.

"Oh, stop," says my mother. "You don't need to worry about the Mafia."

"This is a large city," I say. "And that's where the Mafia work and live."

Just then, a big van with colored windows pulls up alongside the bus and swerves until it is just in front of the bus. The bus lurches to a stop. My mother grabs her purse and hugs it to her chest. I look carefully to see if the Mafia are going to get out of the van and come in and rob us. But what happens is not the Mafia getting out of the van. What happens is that the running man gets out of the van. He sprints over to the door of the bus and gets on. The whole bus cheers and applauds.

"Why would the Mafia care about a running man?" I ask my mother.

"Hush," she says. "That was probably just a soccer mom taking pity."

I do not know how she comes to these illogical conclusions. My mother does not base her thinking on evidence.

When we get to the hotel, I do not like the smell of our room and it takes me some time to choose whether I will sleep on the bed or the couch. Finally, I select the couch. Then my mother calls Alan Phoenix to tell him about the change of plans. Her voice is in the red zone for part of the time, and while she talks I sit beside her and keep opening and shutting the clasp of her purse until she brushes my hand away. I am not feeling happy with this part of the trip and I don't want to sit beside her, but I do it anyway. Maybe this is what the new minister back home meant when he came to preach his guest sermon, before the congregation decided to hire him. In times of transition, he said, we look for islands of stability. Islands of stability. I didn't understand it then but I think I do now. In this new hotel room, my mother and her flowered purse are an island of stability, even though I don't want them to be.

We spend the night in the hotel and then we go to the restaurant in the airport for breakfast. I have pancakes and I ask for blueberries, but the waitress says they don't have any. This is disappointing and I fill out the little card on the table where it asks for customer comments: *Should get blueberries,* I write. That will be smart information for them so that they can prepare for next time.

Arriving in France

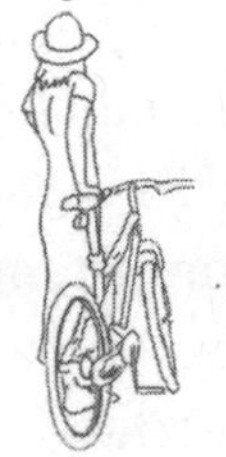

On July 5 we fly overnight from New York to Frankfurt, where the time goes forward by five hours. Then we run through the airport for thirty-seven minutes and then we get onto a shuttle bus that takes us to the airplane going to Marseille. This is a day that has too much flying in it. The first flight takes eight hours and thirty minutes. The second flight takes one hour and fifty-seven minutes. My mother says if Alan Phoenix isn't there to meet us she is going to kill him, but I don't think she means it. Killing is against the law. And anyway, he is her boyfriend.

Alan Phoenix is there to meet us and he has the rented car outside, but there is an important problem. The problem isn't Alan Phoenix and the car. The problem is that our luggage does not come off the plane after us. We have to wait for a baggage attendant who speaks English to come back from her coffee break. She tells us that our bags are coming on the next flight and that they will be delivered to our home after 5 PM that evening. I do not want to leave the airport without my suitcase, but my mother says to get in the car and count to a hundred. Counting to a hundred isn't nearly long enough. When I am tired of counting, I start chewing gum. What I am thinking of is all the things in my suitcase and how each time I want them they will not be there and so everything will change.

In particular, I will miss my alarm clock. I love my alarm clock. It has an entirely predictable face. It stands on four little legs and you can hear the ticking so you know it's working. It was broken once, and Danny my mother's ex-boyfriend said, "Too bad it can't ever be fixed." But he was wrong. Even after I threw it against a wall and the glass front fell off, he was still wrong. A watchmaker got it working again. The case is a nice sky-blue and the clock face is white. I've had it ever since I was a little kid. There's a toggle on the back that you have to crank every night. It works on the principle of springs, which unwind according to schedule if they are tightened in the opposite direction. Mom has stopped talking about getting me a new one because she knows what I will say. And I don't want a new one now.

Now we are taking the A51 autoroute, and going through a gate, getting a ticket, and then driving along a straight road that Alan Phoenix says is a toll road. But apparently it's the wrong road, and we can't get off it. He is usually a quiet person but all at once his voice goes into the red zone. "Watch for a place to turn around!" he says.

It is frightening to be on a road and unable to escape. My hands are wet with sweat. My mother keeps turning around and trying to talk to me but I can't tell what she is saying. We drive for a long time. Finally, there is a place to turn off, and another road that we can take to go back. Soon we're driving in the opposite direction on the straight road.

"What about my shampoo?" I say finally, through dry lips. "I won't have any shampoo and I can't wash my hair, and then I can't go out because you're not supposed to show your grease to other people. And if I can't go out, I probably can't babysit Martin Phoenix and then Alan Phoenix will fire me."

Alan Phoenix turns around and you're not supposed to turn around when you are driving and he says something in yelling that sounds like, "I'm not going to fire you!" But I can't tell if he really said that or if he's just talking about firewood.

I take a deep breath and then I take another. I think about my two gerbils, Harold Pinter and Samuel Beckett, safe in their cage at Shauna's house and not eating each other. I look out the window and see that the sky is all blue. There are no clouds anywhere and the whole sky is very big here. This is comforting because I like the sky, and I do not like clouds. Clouds are always changing. I take another deep breath.

"And we have lots of shampoo at the villa!" Alan Phoenix says.

"It's not worth breaking the car," I say. "Stop turning around and stay looking toward the road. And stop putting your voice in the red zone."

Just as I say that, a driver passes us from behind and I see him reach out his right hand and show his middle finger. That is a very bad word to show to anyone.

"Never mind," mutters Alan Phoenix. "People around here drive too fast."

It is good that he is not yelling anymore.

We pass through a toll gate and have to pay. Then we are back in Marseille again, looking for the right road. Alan Phoenix heaves a big sigh and we turn onto a road that looks different from the one we took earlier.

"This is the one we want!" he says.

I see that the fields on both sides of the road are flat. Instead of wheat or barley like we have in Canada near Saskatoon, the crops are something else with very green leaves.

"What's growing out there?" I ask.

"Grapes," says Alan Phoenix. His thin blond hair is stuck to his head and I think he has been sweating. It is good he is not yelling anymore. "These are vineyards, and you can see green or red grapes on the vines," he says. "In September they'll be harvested and made into wine."

"Stop the car!" I say. "I need to take a photograph of this!"

"We don't need to stop now," my mother says. "Let's just get to the villa."

"It's okay," says Alan Phoenix. "I could use a drink of water anyways." Alan Phoenix stops the car on the side of the road, and I get out and take a picture for my photo album. Alan Phoenix finds his water bottle in the trunk and takes a long swallow. I watch as his Adam's apple goes up and down. I have noticed that tall skinny men always have big Adam's apples.

Later, we pass a field of something purple.

"What's growing out there?" I ask.

"Lavender," says Alan Phoenix. "People harvest lavender

for its oil. You've probably smelled it in bath salts or maybe in perfume."

"It would probably give me a headache," I say. "But I like the color. Stop the car!"

"Taylor, you have the whole summer to take pictures!" says my mother. "We want to get to our villa and unpack!"

"We don't have anything to unpack," I remind her. Alan Phoenix stops the car on the side of the road and I get out to take a photograph of the boxes the lavender will be packed in after it is picked.

"Is anyone hungry?" he asks.

"I am," I say.

"Good!" he says. "I was hoping you were because I missed breakfast. Okay if we stop for lunch, Penny?" He looks at my mother. "Penny for your thoughts?" he says. She sighs and then smiles.

"Okay," says my mother. "But let's not stop for too long."

In thirty-two minutes, we stop at an outdoor restaurant for lunch. The menu is written in French and my mother and I cannot understand it.

"Is this duck?" my mother asks, pointing at something on the menu.

The waitress cannot understand our English.

"Try sign language," says Alan Phoenix to my mother. "Quack, quack." He flaps his arms and grins at the waitress. She nods.

"Quack, quack," she repeats. "Oui. Canard."

It is clear my mother does not want to try to speak to the waitress in French or in sign language. She just points at things on the menu to place her order. Alan Phoenix orders in French. So do I, by copying part of what he says.

"Crêpes, s'il vous plaît," I say. My mother gets some kind of a salad that looks as if it has raw bacon on top. Alan Phoenix gets an omelet. I get a crepe with butter and sugar and I eat it all.

"I thought my high-school French would come back to me, but it hasn't," Mom says to him. "Nobody will be able to understand me here."

"Give it time. You just need to take chances. People will forgive you for making mistakes, but they can't forgive you if you don't try," he says.

I did not take French in high school at all, because I had to take Special Education. From reading a translation book, I have learned some French words and I try using them on the waitress.

"Merci beaucoup," I say when she fills my water glass, pronouncing each letter as carefully as I can.

"Merci," she replies, and I think I have done it right.

My mother's mouth curves up and then she turns her head the other way. Alan Phoenix asks for the bill. He tells us that waiters here think it is impolite to bring the bill unless you ask, in case you are interested in staying longer. He checks to see if he can use his credit card and then he pays. My mother could pay for us because she has the money from Grandma's will, but she does not.

As we leave the restaurant, I ask when my job with Martin Phoenix is going to start, and Alan Phoenix says that it will start tomorrow and that after supper I can hang out and get used to the routines here.

"I will hang out with Luke Phoenix and Martin Phoenix,

but I will not hang out any windows," I say, just to show him I understand what he is talking about.

I am excited about my new job starting tomorrow. I like Martin Phoenix and I have hung out with him in Saskatoon enough to know what he likes and does not like. His favorite activities are science and art, and he can navigate the keyboard of his Tango—a speech communication device that talks for him. He can also feed himself, as long as he has enough time and someone to help him clean up.

I am proud to put this babysitting job on my resumé because it will make me seem important to have worked in France. When I get back to Saskatoon, other employers will see that I have worked in three places: Waskesiu, Saskatoon, and France. I hope this will make me more employable. And being employable means something great: being independent.

The Lost Luggage

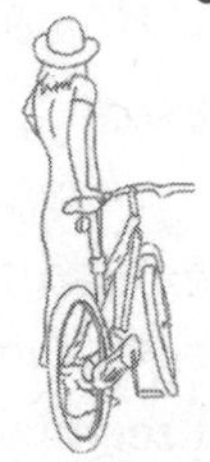

At 5 PM that first evening in France, I look out the window of our villa and I do not see a baggage delivery truck, or a van, or even a car. All I see are the cherry trees in the front yard, and then the olive trees, and beyond these the vineyards, with the blue Luberon mountains in the distance. I thought that we would be staying in a town called Lourmarin, but we are in the countryside.

"They're not coming," I say.

"Give them time," my mother says. "They'll come."

But they don't. We eat supper, Alan Phoenix, my mother, Luke Phoenix, Martin Phoenix, and me, sitting around a table outside the back door. On the table is a long skinny loaf of bread called a baguette, a plate of different kinds of cheese, a bowl of olives, and dishes of meatloaf, cooked carrots, and mashed potatoes. There is also a bottle of wine and a pitcher of water with lemons floating inside.

Beside Martin Phoenix are smaller bowls that contain his portions; he has his carrots mashed in with his potatoes and wheat germ added to make it healthier. He also has his meatloaf mixed together with cheese. I am not hungry for anything.

"Try the goat cheese," Martin Phoenix says slowly with his Tango computer. "It's good. The blue cheese is gross. It's from sheep."

This kind of Tango is not a dance. It is a speech device that helps Martin Phoenix talk. It was invented by the father of another child with cerebral palsy, and it looks like a Game Boy but it is not a Game Boy. The screen has subjects arranged by icons, and when you press the icon, you go into lists of words from which you can create phrases or sentences. Then the Tango talks for you, using a recorded voice. Martin Phoenix's "voice" sounds like a thirteen-year-old boy, because that is what he is, and he would not want to sound like a woman or a man.

"Roquefort, gross? Mmmm, my favorite," says Alan Phoenix, helping himself to a big chunk. "Thank you, 'ewe'!"

I don't know what he is talking about but I try a tiny crumb of the blue cheese. Martin Phoenix is right. It is gross. I spit it out on my plate and Martin Phoenix makes laughing sounds, which he can do without his Tango. Then we hear a bird calling from the nearby trees. "Cuck-oo, cuck-oo."

" 'Sing on, sing on, you gray-brown bird,' " quotes Luke Phoenix. " 'Sing from the swamps, the recesses, pour your chant from the bushes.' Walt Whitman, 1865."

The cuckoo waits for a moment as if it has heard him, and

then it calls again. I count the units of birdsong. Seven.

Luke Phoenix eats an olive and then spits the pit at his brother. He hits him in the head. Luke Phoenix says, "Hot cross buns!" and Martin Phoenix uses his Tango to say, "Bastard."

"Stop using bad words," says Alan Phoenix to his youngest son, "or I'll take away that Tango and you'll just have to use thought transference." He is smiling when he says that last part, so I don't think he means it.

At 5:20 PM, I go and look into the front yard. There is no luggage vehicle coming up the driveway.

"It'll come, Taylor, don't worry!" says Alan Phoenix.

"I have extra clothes here if you need to borrow anything," says Luke Phoenix.

"Do you have a jean dress?" I ask. That is what I am missing most of all out of my suitcase. My mother convinced me to wear pants on the airplane, and now I have no jean dress.

"Ha ha," says Luke Phoenix. "Very funny."

"His jean dress is in the wash," says Martin Phoenix with his Tango.

There is ice cream for dessert, and although I haven't eaten any main course I try some of the ice cream. It is coconut, although its label just says *Coco*. Martin Phoenix gets his with skim-milk powder stirred into it. When he's finished the milk and ice cream, Alan Phoenix wipes his son's face and hands and then they go to the bathroom where Martin Phoenix has his teeth brushed. I pay close attention because tomorrow after breakfast I will be doing these things with Martin Phoenix.

I look out the window at 5:40. No luggage.

"Taylor, come and take your mind off our suitcases," says my mother. "We can get all sorts of TV channels here, English as well as French, but I don't know how to use the remote."

"How could a mind be on a suitcase?" I ask, coming out of the bathroom. My mother doesn't answer. She just hands me the remote.

"All the instructions are in French," she says.

I do not want to watch television. It makes me mad that my mother expects me to figure out how to use it when I'm not the one who wants to watch. But I look at the universal symbols on the remote and activate the television.

"Whose turn is it to do the dishes?" calls Alan Phoenix, who is still in the bathroom with Martin Phoenix.

"Not mine!" says Luke Phoenix.

"Taylor, you could lend a hand," my mother tells me. "This family is kind enough to invite you to France—the least you can do is the dishes."

"I was hired to babysit," I say, "not clean. Cleaning is what I'm trying to get away from."

"Taylor, just go and do the dishes!" my mother says. Her voice is quickly going up the loudness scale.

"I thought you wanted me to figure out how to use the television!" I say. She grabs the remote from my hand.

"I can do it from here," she says, which is confusing. She is sitting in the same spot she was sitting in five minutes ago.

Luke Phoenix goes and checks a piece of paper on the fridge.

"It's your turn, Dad. Excellent! Martin and I are going to play boules on the driveway. Taylor, wanna come?"

"What are boules?" I ask.

"Come on, I'll show you," he says.

I leave my mother with the television and go outside. Boules is a game where players each have two silver balls. You take turns throwing them to see who can be closest to a small green rubber ball that the first player throws away from where everyone is standing. You get a point if you are the closest with one ball, and two points if both your balls are the closest.

I am the first to get twenty points, which we count in French. "Vingt!" Martin Phoenix announces on his Tango. Martin Phoenix is second with fifteen: quinze. Luke Phoenix is third with onze. "Eleven is still respectable," he says. "Anything over 'dix' is decent." After we put the balls away in the garage, we walk by some sunflowers growing by the back door.

" 'Ah, Sunflower! weary of time,' " quotes Luke Phoenix.

"What?" Martin asks with his Tango. And then in French: "Quoi?" The French voice on the Tango sounds a lot like Luke Phoenix's voice.

"Who programmed it in French?" I ask Luke Phoenix.

"I did," he says. "On the airplane. 'Ah, Sunflower! weary of time,' " he repeats. "William Blake, 1794. 'Who countest the steps of the Sun/Seeking after that sweet golden clime/ Where the traveler's journey is done ...' "

Luke Phoenix often quotes poetry. I don't know why he does it. I Googled this passage by William Blake so I could get the line lengths right, in case that makes a difference. At first I didn't know what the words meant, but now I do. I am just as weary of time as that sunflower. I go inside to the front window and look out. Still no luggage. It is 6:30.

"Shouldn't we call them on the phone?" I ask.

My mother is fiddling with channels on the television.

"Mom?"

"Well, I did try, but all there is now is an answering message in French," she says. "The luggage will come tomorrow morning."

But the next morning the luggage does not come! I look out the window while my mother sleeps in. The rest of them have biked to town to buy groceries, because Alan Phoenix is not painting today. He says my job will start tomorrow. Alan Phoenix has rented a special cart that rides behind his bicycle and today Martin Phoenix sits inside it. Luke Phoenix rides another bike. There is a third bike in the garage that I can use if I want. It is the white bicycle and I do want to ride it sometime. Just not today.

I walk around the villa and look in all the cupboards and drawers. Then I open the windows because the air in the house is stuffy from the night. The windows are just single panes of glass and they have no screens. I hope nothing flies in when they are open. Then I look at the bookshelf in my room and take out a small gray book by Jean-Paul Sartre. The cover is soft and I like the feel of it in my hands. The phone rings three times while I am looking at the book, but I don't answer it.

Finally, I get so tired of waiting for our luggage that I call the number on the sheet my mother was given at the airport and I talk to the woman who answers. She understands some English and she tells me the luggage has been in the van since yesterday, but the driver can't find our house. Apparently he has tried to phone us several times, but no one answered. "Are you in Lourmarin?" she asks.

"No," I say. "We're in the countryside. It's a villa called Le Colombier." The woman gives me the phone number of the driver and I telephone him. He does not speak English. I am glad I have written down some French sentences that I have translated with the help of my laptop

"Il est difficile de trouver notre maison?" I ask. *Is it difficult to find our house?*

"Oui," says the man.

"Voulez-vous nous rencontrer quelque part en ville?" *Do you want to meet us somewhere in town?*

"Oui," says the man. "Rencontrez-moi à l'église de Vaugines en une heure."

"What?" I say. "Quoi?"

"Onze heures," says the man. There is a pause. He goes on. "Time. Onze heures. Vaugines. Église. Oui?"

"Oui," I answer. "Merci."

I hang up the phone. I tell my mother I have arranged to meet the person who has our baggage in Vaugines at 11 AM.

"Where in Vaugines?" she asks, standing up.

"I don't know," I answer. "Just wait, I have to look it up."

I type various spellings of "église" into my laptop and eventually get the answer. "It's the church!" I yell.

"Where is the church in Vaugines?" she calls back.

I have no idea and all Google can tell me is that the church is at the edge of the village. We get into the car and my mother uses bad language.

"I don't like driving here," she says. "And this car is a standard. Hang on."

"What should I hang on to?" I ask, but she doesn't answer.

In seconds we are careering down the driveway and onto the road, heading toward Vaugines.

When Alan Phoenix was driving, I did not notice how narrow the roads in France are or how close the other cars come to us when they arrive from the opposite direction. Sometimes, my mother has to pull off the road onto what little space there is, to avoid being hit. Twice somebody shows us the middle finger when they pass us from behind. When we drive ahead of two cyclists attempting to turn onto the road, one of them pushes the back of his fingers under his chin and brushes them forward at us. I'm not sure what this means but I think it's something rude.

My mother swears when he does this and the car bounces forward. I don't know why she is driving a standard when she doesn't know how.

"You should not drive this car," I say. "And you should not say those words."

"Never mind," she says. "Just look for the church." I do not see anything that looks like my church back home. Then my mother pulls into a parking lot by a big stone building. There is a bell at the top of one of its towers. There is another vehicle in the parking lot. It is a van.

I do not want to get out of our car. I do not want to see what is in that van in case it is *not* our suitcases. Anything could be in there. Even the Mafia.

"Let's go," says my mother.

I close my eyes.

"Taylor, don't be ridiculous," she says, and exits the car. I open my eyes a crack and peek out at the van. Inside, I see a white-haired man and a white-haired woman. The back door of the van is open. I see the fabric of suitcases.

I take a deep breath and open my door. The man with white hair gets out of the van. He waves at us and my mother waves back, even though you are not supposed to wave at strangers.

The man goes around to the back of the van. I get out of the car, put one foot after the other, and follow my mother.

There is my suitcase on the pavement! I am so glad to see it that I run over and hug it to my chest. Then I open it and some underwear falls out, but I find my little blue and white alarm clock and it is still working.

"Taylor," my mother is saying to me in a low voice. "Do you think we have to pay?"

"Est-il possible de payer avec une carte de crédit?" I ask the man. This is what I heard Alan Phoenix asking at the restaurant yesterday after we had lunch.

"Non, je vous remercie. C'est déjà payé." I don't understand any of this except for "non." The man smiles and shakes his head and climbs back into the driver's seat. I wave because he is not a stranger any more—and now I have my suitcase, which makes me very delighted.

I watch my mother put her suitcase into our car and then I do the same, and she slams down the trunk. She does not look happy.

"Are you feeling okay?" I ask.

"I can't communicate properly here," she says. "I do know some French words, but I just can't seem to think of them when I need them. It makes me feel ... I don't know ... childish ... inadequate."

"Being able to communicate is an art and a craft," I tell

her, and she looks at me with a strange expression. This is something Shauna used to say to me at school and I think it means that communication takes work.

We drive home a little faster, with no bumps or swearing. Just before we turn into our lane, we pass a bus stop. The shelter is the same shape as the bus stops at home.

My First Day of Work

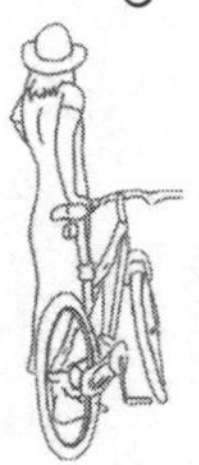

I am excited about my first morning of work and everything goes well. Martin Phoenix and I make lunch for everyone and while we are sitting out under the umbrella in the back yard, potter wasps are attracted to the food. When all we have left to eat is dessert, we go inside. It is crème brûlée and we made it by baking a custard base of cream, vanilla, eggs, and sugar, and then burning sugar on top by putting the dish under the grill. My mother says I should really think of becoming a chef, but I think she should just shut up about that.

My favorite foods are pancakes and hamburgers, even though I didn't want to eat a hamburger once with a boyfriend I met last summer. At least I think he was my boyfriend. There were two boyfriends then, one for a few days, and one for just a few minutes. I hope soon I will collect another boyfriend who likes me and who I like, and that the relationship lasts longer than it did with those two.

I like the crème brûlée, even if Martin Phoenix told everyone it was called poop pie.

This afternoon, I get the white bicycle out of the garage and follow the lane. I pass the garbage cans. I pass the recycling unit. I pass a green wire fence and see that clusters of small white snails have gathered on the top of each post.

I stop the bicycle and go over for a closer look. I wonder why they have chosen this particular fence to climb. I wonder why they went to the highest points possible on the fence and why they are gathered together. Maybe they are mating. It seems disrespectful to look at them, if they are doing some kind of group sex, but I study them for a minute more before I go. Most of them seem to know the rules about clustering as high as possible, but there are a few snails lower down on the fence that haven't caught up to the others. I feel sad for them but I leave them there. They will find their way. I am sure of it. They just might take a little longer than the rest.

I see some red and white marks on the trees and decide that when I get back I will ask Luke Phoenix what these mean. If he does not know, I will ask Alan Phoenix, and if he does not know, I will ask Martin Phoenix. If none of them know, I will not ask my mother. I am tired of asking her things because sometimes she just doesn't answer, and sometimes she talks too much.

I think again about how a mind could be on a suitcase and suddenly I get it. You can make up your mind, which means you can make a decision, just like you can put your mind down on something, which means resting it there and thinking about a topic for longer than a few seconds. And while you are resting your mind, someone can ask you, "Penny for your thoughts?" just like Alan Phoenix said to my mother, even if your name isn't Penny, which hers is.

The Red-and-White Trail

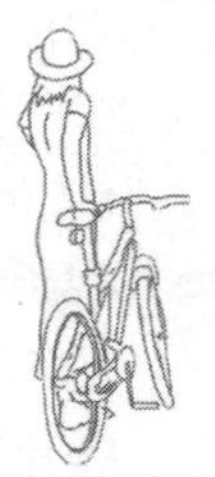

The first week in France went by very quickly. Things are so different here. Even the sheets smell different, because they are hung on the clothesline to dry, and at first I had trouble sleeping. I am glad that I am finally getting used to things. On my second Sunday here, I take the white bicycle out of the garage and I ride past the cherry trees and down the driveway, just as I have done before. It is good that some things stay the same. It is a warm July afternoon, but when I am riding, the air feels cool and fresh. I go down the lane toward the woods, and I see the red and white lines on the trees. Luke Phoenix told me that these lines mark a hiking trail.

I follow the red-and-white trail and it leads me into the forest on a path that changes from gravel to dirt. There are tree roots and rocks that make the path difficult to ride on, so I begin to carry the white bicycle, telling myself all the while that the road will get better up ahead. The path descends through an old stream bed and then up and around huge tree roots that I struggle to navigate. Rocks are strewn along the way and I keep stumbling, but going forward, agonizing over my decision to continue. Shall I retrace my steps? Shall I go on? Just a little further, I keep thinking. The path will get better up ahead.

Heat from the sun is falling through the thin leaves of the olive trees and my skin hurts. The cicadas are singing their electric song.

Off to the left, I encounter an older couple. One of them is sitting on a fallen log in the shade, and the other is standing in a ray of light.

"Bonjour," I say, and the one standing nods.

"Bonjour."

They seem to be waiting for someone, I think, but I know they aren't waiting for Godot, like the people in Samuel Beckett's play. Sometimes, I feel like I'm waiting like that and I don't know what I'm waiting for, and it's not a nice feeling. It's a panicky feeling. It's a feeling that makes me want to swear and obsessively clean things, just like I'm trying not to do.

After I say hello, I carry the white bicycle past the two people in the woods and keep going forward, and the path grows more and more difficult, and I can hear my breath rattling in my chest. Just a little further, I keep telling myself. Scaling a sharp ridge, I fall and scrape my shin, and then finally I come to a stop. What if the path does not get better? What if I shouldn't have come into this forest in the first place? I can feel the white-out rising behind my eyes. I don't know what to do next.

Go back. That is the best choice. I toil through the white haze that clouds my vision and start back, sweat dripping down my neck from the heat of my long hair. This time, the couple are both in the shade, one still on the log, the other stretched out on the ground. I take a deep breath and the haze clears.

"Bonjour," I say, my voice cracking. "Bonjour," I repeat.

They do not answer. It is possible they are asleep, except that I think the person on the log is eating pistachio nuts. It is also possible that they are confused by the way I am carrying the white bicycle back and forth in the forest, and perhaps there is ridicule in their gaze. I don't know why but I feel hotter as I pass. I feel them looking at me, judging me. *Look at her, there. The Freaker.* Voices echo from the past and I wonder if I'll ever stop hearing them. I wish I could climb out of my skin and be somewhere else. The heat is terrible, and in the end I'm not sure I am on the same path as before. Even the stream bed, once I come to it, looks different.

But I emerge from the forest and put the white bicycle down on the gravel road, slip onto the seat, and put my feet to the pedals. Soon the wind is at my back and I skim along home, lost and then found. C'est la vie. *Such is life.*

My Daily Schedule

I am the only one who doesn't mind getting up early, and so the morning part of Martin Phoenix's day is my responsibility. We have a regular routine that we follow here at the villa. Alan Phoenix has washed and shaved by the time Martin Phoenix finishes his meal, and usually they go out into the yard looking for ripe figs while I do the dishes: theirs and mine from breakfast, and anything left over from last night when the five of us—Alan Phoenix, Luke Phoenix, Martin Phoenix, my mother, and I—had our bedtime snacks. Five of us can use a lot of dishes, even just at bedtime.

After Alan Phoenix goes next door to work with Madame Colombe, his partner in an art project he is working on here in France, Martin Phoenix and I go for a walk anywhere that his wheelchair will allow, or else we play checkers, or work on paintings of our own. Martin Phoenix can paint with his fingers and I print the title of his work underneath. His painting this morning was called *Garden Poop* and consisted of various splotches of brown. In the corner of the page was a large gray figure that I thought was a pigeon but he said was his brother, my friend Luke Phoenix.

I met Luke Phoenix last fall in a biology class at the University of Saskatchewan. We are the same age because I failed kindergarten and he failed a different grade after his mother died and his brother was born with cerebral palsy and had to be taken to various clinics all over the United States. Although Luke Phoenix is my friend, he could also be my brother someday if my mother and his father get married, but even though we are the same age we would not be twins. If my mother and his father get married, that would make Martin Phoenix my brother as well. If Martin Phoenix were my brother, I could not put this babysitting/personal care job on my resumé because you can't get a professional credit by working for your own family. I hope that my mother will not make any changes to our group dynamics until we get home to Canada and my work here is finished. Otherwise, my resumé will be ruined.

Usually Alan Phoenix comes back home for lunch and by this time my mother is awake and Luke Phoenix has returned from his tennis lesson. We all have bread and cheese—there are many kinds of cheeses here to choose from—and sometimes my mother and Alan Phoenix even have wine, which is not appropriate for lunch. They defend themselves by saying it is customary in France to have a small glass at noon. I did not know wine habits could be different between two countries.

We also have olives and fruit for lunch, as they grow all

through the Luberon Valley. Peaches are in season and sometimes there are figs. I do not like the olives or peaches, but the figs are quite pleasant, with centers rather like blueberries when they are neither too sour nor too sweet. Luke Phoenix likes to eat olives and then spit the pits at his brother. He has a surprisingly good aim. When a pit hits Martin Phoenix he wriggles in his chair and then Luke Phoenix says, "Hot cross buns!" and Martin Phoenix calls Luke Phoenix bad names using his Tango, just as he has done before. I don't know what hot cross buns have to do with anything.

Sometimes, while we are eating, there are silences, and my friend Luke Phoenix usually fills those silences with quotations. Sometimes he talks to the cuckoo we hear in the trees, calling out to it: "'Sing on there in the swamp/O singer bashful and tender. I hear your notes, I hear your call, I hear, I come presently, I understand you ...' Walt Whitman, 1865." I don't know why he does this. The cuckoo cannot understand him.

At other times when there are silences, my mother fills them by trying to give me advice. She is continually telling me what to do. Lately, she has been talking a lot about my jean dress. My jean dress, she says, is disgustingly old and should be thrown away. She has also been talking a lot about cooking classes. She thinks I should take a cooking class and learn some professional skills. She also thinks that I should get a card for the public library in Vaugines and see if they have any film nights where I would meet nice young people. Film nights? Nice young people?

I told her that Martin Phoenix and Luke Phoenix were

nice young people and that I was happy associating with them. That's when our conversation got kind of confusing. My mother said that because she and Alan Phoenix were a couple, even though they weren't married, Martin Phoenix and Luke Phoenix were kind of like my brothers.

"Not really my brothers," I clarified, because I want to put the job of personal care assistant on my resumé.

"They are not really your brothers," she said. "But they could be someday. So I don't want you getting ideas about Luke Phoenix, even though he is your age and you like him and spend a lot of time with him. You should be out meeting lots of other teens your age."

I do not know what she meant about Luke Phoenix, so I am specifically writing that part down here. Maybe I will be able to figure it out if I think more about it. I wonder if my mother should be out meeting more people *her* age. Is consistency of age an important quality among friends? Sometime at lunch or dinner I will ask my mother about that. I like to ask her questions at lunch or dinner so that if she starts to talk too long, she will get hungry and stop talking. My mother seems to like the food here a great deal.

The deli ham is disgusting—all slimy and full of fat. Also disgusting is the baking that comes from the markets where there are flies and other bugs. I saw a wasp crawling out of a hole in a honey pretzel just before someone bought it. Once Alan Phoenix brought home pigeon eggs, but I did not eat them. Pigeon eggs would be especially disgusting. I have seen what the pigeons eat around here.

In the afternoons I usually go for a walk or a bike ride, but sometimes we all go sightseeing instead. One afternoon we drove through the Luberon Mountains to Apt and then over to Isle sur la Sorgue, and then to Fontaine de Vaucluse where there was supposed to be a special fountain, but it wasn't very interesting.

We ate in a restaurant and I had crepes with butter and sugar, even though my mother tried to get me to order something containing a vegetable. Alan Phoenix and my mother had onion soup, and Luke Phoenix had duck basted with honey, garlic, and thyme, as well as creamed zucchini. Alan Phoenix asked him if he had brought his wallet. Martin Phoenix had chef's crepes, which had cheese, ham, and an egg on top, and then he had pistachio ice cream with a hair in it. The waitress told us that she came from a family with eight brothers and four sisters and she was proud to say that they all worked in restaurants. She herself has two children and is very happy with that number.

"Mais vous semblez très heureuse avec trois enfants, Madame," she told my mother, holding up three fingers. My mother got all red and flustered. She had understood enough to know that the waitress thought Martin Phoenix, Luke Phoenix, and I were all her children. That would only be true if my mother and Alan Phoenix got married, and all I can say is that this better not happen this summer.

"Do you offer cooking classes?" my mother asked the waitress in English and then Alan Phoenix translated it into French. I can see the scene now as if it is a movie replaying in my head.

"Non," says the waitress, shaking her head.

"Too bad, because my daughter would like to take one," my mother says.

"No, I would not!" I say, with my voice loud enough to be in the red zone. But sometimes it is as if my mother is stone deaf.

"We'll see," she says.

The room starts to look white and I feel hot with my anger. But I think about sending the anger down through my body, away from my head and into my feet. This takes the whiteness away with it, and I can see in colors again. I do not like to cook. I have never liked to cook. And I am not going to learn to cook French food!

Tuesday August 5

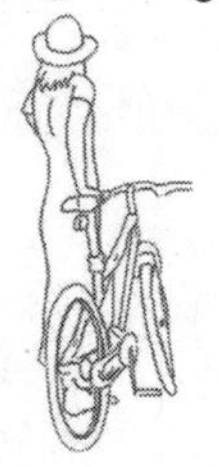

This afternoon it is raining, so we are not sightseeing, and I am not going for my usual walk or bike ride. I am sitting at my big desk overlooking the yard and working on this journal. My mother is shopping after making me promise—three times, as if I'm a stupid baby—not to go outside in the rain without my raincoat. Alan Phoenix has driven Martin Phoenix to the doctor because Martin Phoenix has some kind of rash, and Luke Phoenix has gone along because he knows some of the French that his father does not.

Through the large window of my bedroom I can see the cherry trees, and beyond them a grove of olive trees, and beyond that the vineyards across the road. Past the vineyards are the tree-covered Luberon mountains, which today are shrouded with mist. The sound of the rain on the tile roof shingles of the villa makes me feel sleepy, but I open the desk drawer and take out some cinnamon gum. Peppermint would be calming and organizing but cinnamon wakes me up. My mother read about gum on an autism website and, unlike much of her advice, I find the gum to be very helpful.

Today I need to start thinking about my earliest memories and find the ones I want to include in this journal. It is easy for me to remember things. The problem is that some of the things I remember, I wish I could forget.

My Earliest Memory

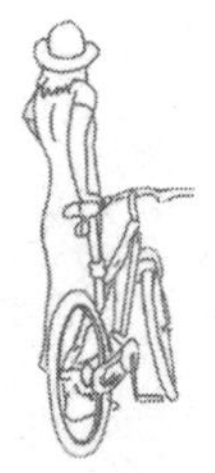

I am four years old. I have long dark hair and blue eyes, just as I do now. My father is walking me to kindergarten for the first time and the sidewalk has yellow dandelions coming up through cracks in the cement. My father says, "Look at all the yellow buttons on the sidewalk," but I do not see any buttons. I do not know why we are going to school, and I do not know yet that he will leave me there.

In the classroom, I see four round red tables, sixteen small green chairs, a large brown desk with a big brown chair, a blue carpet, a brown rocking chair, a shelf of books, and bins of toys. I go to the bin that contains toy cars and begin lining them up on the edge of the carpet. It is important to get them in a straight line but every time I am almost finished, another kid comes along and moves one. I am concentrating hard on what I am doing and for a while I don't see who is moving the cars, so at first I keep thinking that it is my fault when the line is not straight. When I do see a kid pick up a car, I am so full of rage that I start throwing the cars all over the place. A woman comes and grabs my hands. Her mouth is moving but I can't tell what she is saying. Someone is screaming and it is so loud in here. Maybe the person screaming is me.

Someone is taking me out of the classroom and talking at me in gibberish. I grab anything within reach and throw it, because I don't know where I am being taken. I look around for my father but he is gone. That is when I start to kick and everything goes white, like a screen at the end of a movie.

After a long time, my mother is there. She takes me from whomever is holding me and sits with me for a while until I have caught my breath and start to see in colors again. Then we go home.

This scene at school replays itself for many days. If it weren't for the fact that going to kindergarten always ended with me lost in a meltdown, it would have been almost comforting in its repetition: I go to kindergarten; I line up the cars; I have a meltdown and everything goes white; my mother takes me home. But it is not comforting. It is exhausting to be so angry and then, later, to become aware of being in a new situation different from the one that made me mad. As if everything has been erased and then replaced with something unfamiliar. Week after terrible week. And all the time I don't have the right words to make anyone else understand how I am feeling.

My mother is sitting on a chair at the back of the classroom. I can see her sitting there while I am playing with the cars. I look at her every now and then, and I know that she is my mother because I recognize the flowered handbag she always carries. "That is really my mother," I keep saying to myself. I am glad she is here. When another child takes one of my cars, I open my mouth and yell. I am surprised that my mother does not come over and get it back, but she does not, and I yell harder. I yell until my mother does come over, but she just picks me up and takes me back to her chair. We sit there and I kick her every now and then, just to give her the message that I want that car back, until finally she wraps her legs around mine and I am wedged tightly onto her lap. I begin to breathe deeply and I can feel my eyelids closing. My mother is what the minister would call an island of stability. But I know I am not supposed to sleep here. I look drowsily at all the colors around us and slide off my mother's lap. My mother nudges me back toward the cars and I edge over to begin my play again.

The teacher is putting up pictures on the October bulletin board. During the last month I have read all the books on the shelf and now I know better than to play with the cars because somebody always takes one. Today I am sitting at the computer typing random letters. This is best because if I write something intelligible the teacher always wants to talk about it.

A boy comes over. His mouth is moving and sounds are coming out but I don't hear any words. Then he tries to push me out of my chair. I grab the mouse and pull it out of the computer; then I hit him on the side of the head with it. He runs away crying and I sit back down, plug in the mouse, and continue to type random letters.

I am surprised when the teacher comes over and turns off the computer. The computer is always on all day.

"Computer," I say. "On all day."

"It's going to stay off until you apologize to Elton," says the teacher very slowly.

I turn the computer back on, because that's the only way you can type the letters, and when the teacher tries to turn it off, I bite her on the hand.

Then there are a lot of loud voices and soon I am sitting in an office where I see another computer. When the person gets out of the big chair, I go and sit there and then start typing my letters again. I do this until my mother comes and takes me home.

That night my parents yell a lot against each other. I can't tell what they are saying, because they are in their bedroom and the door is shut, but the voices are so loud they make my teeth ache. My skin starts to hurt and I roll myself up in the sheet from my bed. If I roll it tightly enough, the soreness in my skin goes away. Then the yelling comes out of the bedroom and fills the whole house and I am in the middle of it. I am in the middle of the yelling and I can't find any relief.

I am in a little room at school and my mother is sitting on a chair outside the door. I can see a corner of her flowered handbag where it sits near the doorway. There is a person across the table from me and a gray machine on the table, and the machine dangles red, white, and green cords. I am wearing headphones and I am supposed to say "yes" every time I hear a beep.

"Yes," I say. "Yes, yes, yes. Yes." I pause, listening carefully. "Yes."

This goes on for eleven minutes and then we are done.

The person goes outside to talk to my mother and I can hear them whispering.

"Good news. She has normal hearing," the person says.

"I knew her hearing was fine," says my mother. "She hears like a cat."

"Can we get a cat?" I call.

"No," my mother says, coming back into the room and holding out her hand. "Time to go back to the classroom. Come on."

My Second Year in Kindergarten

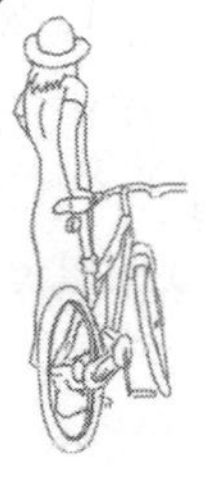

I am five and I am in kindergarten for a second year. Over the weekend, the teacher has put up the October pictures. They are the same pictures she put up last year in 1988. When she asks me to show my mother what I like about the classroom, I select a book from the orange box that she has placed under the bulletin board.

"Bernardo was a little brown bat," I read aloud.

"Oh, Taylor. You must have this book at home," says the teacher.

I look over at my mother. It is frightening to hear the teacher say that she thinks we must get this book. I don't know where we would find it. Will I be punished if we can't find it?

"He lived in a hole in the side of a chestnut tree," I read, my voice shaking a bit. "In the daytime, he slept in his cozy nest. At night, he flew out and ate bugs."

"Very nice reading, Taylor!" says the teacher. "I bet you've read this book so many times you've memorized it!"

I look at the teacher. Everything she says is confusing. I look at my mother.

"Taylor can read," my mother tells the teacher.

"I'm sure she isn't really reading this book," says the teacher. "It's fairly advanced. She's a smart child to memorize things, but she's not a dictionary."

I stand up and go over to the teacher's desk. There is a dictionary on the desk and I pick it up. Of course I am not a dictionary. I am a girl and a dictionary is a book.

"Webster's Dictionary," I read the title, and then go on to read the other words on the cover. "Modern definitions. Easy-to-read type. Parts of speech. More than 440 pages. Specially designed for home, school, and office."

"Oh, my goodness," says the teacher. "I see what you mean. That is quite amazing." The teacher pauses. Then she says, "She does seem academically ready for school. We'll just keep working on the social part. I'm sure being an only child has been difficult, because she won't have had much practice sharing. And she is quite spoiled—you should not give her everything she wants, Mrs. Simon, just because she yells. But not to worry—her social skills will develop. We'll keep working on them and each day is a new day. Right, Taylor?"

I look at the teacher. I have no idea what she is talking about. I look at my mother. She nods. I nod. Then we go home and I hear my mother making sounds in her bedroom that are not happy sounds. I sit naked in a sunbeam until my father gets home and then we have supper.

There is a big amount of yelling in my parents' bedroom. Their voices are so loud I cannot tell one from the other. This frightens me and I squeeze under the couch, where I am pressed between the wooden frame and the cool tile floor. Eventually, I hear some words and I think someone is saying, "And all the buttons are wrecked on the VCR!" But maybe I heard incorrectly even though I know that all the buttons are wrecked—the VCR has not worked in eleven days. I miss the satisfaction of pressing those buttons and seeing something change.

"Don't you tell me I should be a better mother!" someone says. "You should be a better father! How about that?"

I count as high as I can, into the ten thousands, and then I see my father's shoes. He is not supposed to wear them in the house. He is jingling the car keys in his pocket and I come out from under the couch and we go for a drive. We drive past the pet store two times. On the third time we don't go past, we go in, and I ask for a cat. My father says, "No."

"Can I have a small cat or a big cat?" I say. Sometimes if you give people a choice, they pick one of the things that you want instead of none of the things.

"No. No cats."

"A ferret?"

"No."

"Two snakes?"

"No, Taylor. No snakes."

I stand and look at the gerbils for a long time. I don't ask for one but I keep standing there.

"You like those, hey?"

I nod, still looking at them, my hands cupped in front of me as if I am holding one.

"I sense a question in the air," says my father. I do not answer. I do not know what he is talking about.

"Okay. Pick the one you want," my father says finally. "We'll take it home and show your mother."

"Can I have the gerbil to keep?" I ask.

"Yes," he says.

I pick a honey-brown one and the pet-store owner puts it into its own little cage. There are wood shavings on the bottom, and a water bottle, and a little bowl of food.

"What are you going to name it?" asks my father.

"Ashton," I say. There is a little pause.

"No," my father says. "You can't name your gerbil Ashton. That name belongs to ... that was your older brother's name."

"He died," I say. I know that Ashton died a year before I was born so I am not an only child. I don't know why my mother didn't tell this to the teacher. I am not spoiled because I am not an only child.

"You can't use his name for your pet," my father says. "Think of another name. Do you like the name Walnut?"

"Okay," I say. "Walnut."

And when we get home, my parents are not fighting but looking at Walnut, who has already learned to drink water from the little water bottle in the cage. He drinks and drinks and we laugh at the way he holds the water bottle with his paws just like a baby holding a bottle.

Walnut was the first of a series of gerbils. After Walnut came June, and after June came Charlotte, and after Charlotte came Hammy. And last fall, before I turned nineteen, I got my fifth gerbil, Harold Pinter, named after one of my favorite playwrights. Harold Pinter and one of Harold Pinter's babies, Samuel Beckett, are at home in Canada, getting looked after by my friend Shauna and her husband. I hope Harold Pinter doesn't miss me too much or he could get agitated and eat Samuel Beckett. That would be a disaster and I can't bear to think about it. Instead of thinking about it now, I count the birdsong units of the cuckoo that lives in the forest near the villa in France where we are staying. Seven. That is a good number.

I am typing at the kindergarten computer and I type only numbers. Nobody ever tries to talk to me about them when I am typing numbers. Each number has its own personality and I think about the curves and the corners, just as interesting as letters, although other people don't seem to think so. When lined up, numbers have the potential for so many different meanings, just as letters do. Two lines of numbers that are the same length are worth different things if their numbers are different, and it depends on where the round parts are. Six has a round part in the bottom, and it is more than halfway to the most. Eight has two round parts, and it is worth two more than six. Nine has a round part on the top, and it is worth one more than eight. Zero is the biggest round number, and it can make a line of numbers less or more depending on where it is placed. A line of eight sevens is more expensive than a line of eight sixes, but less expensive than a line of nine twos, and a line of nine ones is worth more than any of them if there is a zero at the right end.

Numbers are the smallest unit of meaning I know. Words are the next largest unit of meaning, and in spite of the confusion they often bring, I admire their complexities. Words are almost as interesting as numbers. But it is safer not to use words unless you have to.

Grade One

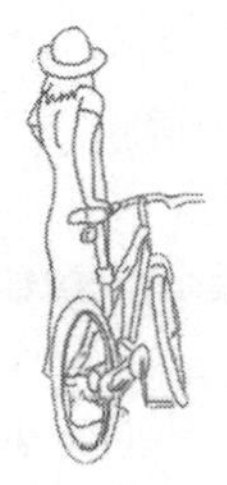

I am finally in grade one. We are supposed to sit on little mats and watch the teacher. It is hard to pay attention to the teacher when there are so many other things in the room to hear and see. The lights buzz. The hot water pipes clang. Noises from the hallway are mysterious and sometimes frightening. The light falls in stripes through the blinds, making the floor seem uneven. I don't like to walk through those stripes in case I stumble, and when I sit on the carpet, I worry about having to get up and walk through the stripes if my teacher says I have to. Bright colors pulse from every corner of the room—from the walls and even from the ceiling where artwork hangs on strings. Compared to these distractions, the teacher is hard to focus on because he moves all the time. It's too much work to look at him even though I know he wants me to.

"Taylor," he is saying. "Taylor Jane, are you paying attention?"

"Yes," I say. This is not a lie. I am paying attention to a lot of things. I know that this is different than paying with money and it makes me feel smart to have sorted this out.

"You have to pay attention or you won't know how to do the work."

I lean over and stroke the back of the kid who is sitting next to me. I don't know if it is a boy or a girl, but he or she often wears a blue sweater that is very soft.

"Mr. Lock, Taylor's touching Jemma's shirt again," says one of the kids.

"I don't mind," says Jemma, sitting very still.

"Go to your desks," says Mr. Lock. "And take out your phonics workbooks. We will do three pages today."

The work is using a pencil to fill in blanks in the book. I don't know why they didn't fill in the blanks when they made the book. Why do we have to do their work for them? Other books come with all the words.

The teacher is right. I do not know the way to fill in the words and I have to erase my work until my pages have holes in them. Everyone else is playing in the Centers, and I am still at my desk erasing numbers. The teacher was angry that I put numbers in where letters are supposed to be. I start to cry. The kid in the blue sweater comes and stands beside my desk, and I reach up and touch the back of the blue sweater. It is so soft and my tears stop coming out.

I am riding my bike without the training wheels. My father is running along beside me, and then suddenly I do not see him any more but I keep going. I bike all the way to the other side of the playground and the wind is in my hair and I am not afraid.

I make a wide turn and come back to where my father is standing. He is breathing heavily and he looks as if he has been sweating. Now my mother is standing there as well. She has the H of wrinkles in the middle of her forehead.

"It's too soon," she is saying. "She could get hurt."

"She's fine," says my father. "And it's not as if there are any cars here. She'll be fine."

My mother turns and walks away. I watch her, and for a few seconds I want to yell at her and tell her not to go. But I start pedalling again.

Then something happens and the bike begins to wobble. I lean over and we fall sideways, the bicycle and I. I scrape my knee and my father comes running over.

"That's not so bad," he says. "Just a little scratch."

I look at my knee. There is a white mark, but no blood.

"Get up and try it again," he says. "Practice makes perfect."

"Practice makes perfect," I say. I like the sound of those words.

The kid in the blue sweater is moving away from Saskatoon to somewhere else and the class has a goodbye party. But I don't want to eat any of the cupcakes and I don't want the kid in the blue sweater to move to another school where I am not going. This time when I put my hand on the back of the sweater, I clutch the fabric. Someone comes and pulls my hand away and then walks with the kid out of the classroom. I try to stand but the teacher holds me in my desk.

In the doorway, the kid in the blue sweater turns and

waves and I think he or she might be waving at me. If the kid in the blue sweater hadn't moved away, he or she would have been my friend. I try to wave back, but the teacher is pushing down on my shoulders.

I can read Mr. Lock's classroom dictionary and it is easier than the one that belonged to the kindergarten teacher. The other kids cluster around when I pick up the grade one dictionary. "Read it!" they demand, and when I do, they mutter among themselves. "She's not really doing it. She's making it up!"

They start bringing things written on pieces of paper for me to read.

"I am a turd," I read, turning over the paper to see if there is anything on the back. There is. "Turn me over and I am still a turd." Someone spins me around and everyone laughs. I am confused. What does it all mean?

I have to stay after school and finish my workbook. This time I put letters in all of the spaces and no numbers. Mr. Lock makes me erase them and start again.

Mr. Lock is standing at the blackboard. He has just asked me a question and I have not answered.

"The sum is right there, Taylor," he says. "Just try and you will see it." His arms wave around and they make me dizzy.

"Five and two ..." he says.

"Seven," I say, surprised at the sudden clarity. Is that what he has been asking me all along? I know all the sums into the triple digits. If he wanted me to tell him the sum of five and two, why didn't he just say so at the beginning?

He taps the blackboard. "Who wants to come and write the answer under the question on the chalkboard?"

A lot of kids put up their hands. I do not. I don't know what Mr. Lock is talking about. Questions are in the air, not on chalkboards.

"Take a strip of colored paper and weave it over and under the strips we have cut in the brown background," says Mrs. Caron, the art teacher. I know that weaving involves wool and a loom. My mother and I have read about this at home. I look around. There are no looms in the classroom. There is no wool, either. I sit and wait for them to bring in the looms and the wool.

"Taylor, please get busy," says Mrs. Caron. "We want to be finished on time."

How can we be on time? I think of Mrs. Caron sitting on the clock. She would squash it for sure. I laugh.

"What's so funny?" asks a kid across the aisle.

"Mrs. Caron is too fat for the clock," I say. Soon I am sitting in an office where that other computer is, and when the person leaves, I type letters. I know better than to type numbers. And this time, I make sure the letters I use spell words. The words I spell are *over and under, over and under, over and under*. These words sound nice. I do not know what they mean but they are kind of like a song.

On the playground there is a big gray metal slide. Kids line up to take turns and I get into line, but when I climb to the top of the slide I don't know the way to do it. What do you do so that you go down?

"Get out of the way!" the kids yell. "Either go down or get out of the way!"

I put one leg on the slide and I see my white skin and my green sock and my brown shoe. I feel like I am going to fall over the edge. The heel of my shoe sticks and makes me wobble. Quickly, I kick the shoe off and it falls down onto the sand. Then I bring the other leg around and take off that shoe as well.

"Taylor's taking off her shoes!" someone yells. "She's throwing them at us!"

I start to go forward and sliding is faster than I thought it would be. I grab the sides of the slide and there is a yell coming out of my throat. I want to go back up but I can't seem to move that way. I feel arms pulling me over the side of the slide and my hands sting. I sniff them. They smell like metal.

Side of the slide, I think. *Side of the slide.*

"You sit on this bench until you're going to play nicely," the person says.

I immediately get up. I am playing nicely.

"Oh no, you don't, not that fast," says the person, pulling me back to the bench. "Sit here for five minutes."

I count to 60 five times and then I get up and go over to the swings. The swings are easy but I keep saying, "Side of the slide," while I am swinging until a kid tells me to stop saying that.

The thing I hate most about grade one are fire drills. Now we are having one. When we have a fire drill, we stop following the schedule and when we stop following the schedule, anything can happen. My mother has told me that other things in my day won't change just because one thing changes, but I don't believe her. One change can make everything else go wrong.

I am standing in the line of kids from my class and I am trying not to cry. My throat hurts and I know that it is because there are sad sounds in there waiting to get out. What if when we get back into our classroom the desks are gone? If my desk is gone, I will have no place to sit and if my things are gone, my parents will be mad. Once I lost a notebook on the way home from school and my mother was really mad.

"They'll think I got rid of it on purpose!" she said after we had driven back and looked all around the parking lot. I don't know why anyone would think she got rid of it on purpose. It has always been my job to carry it. My teacher writes in the notebook every day and when my mother reads it, she sometimes goes into her room and shuts the door. She writes things back, and then in the morning I take the notebook to the teacher. My mother doesn't write very much but the teacher writes at least half a page, and sometimes a full page, and sometimes two pages. The two-page days are when my mother goes into the bedroom and shuts the door.

"Taylor's crying again!" one of the kids says.

I reach up and feel my cheeks, certain that I have not been crying, but my face is wet. My legs shake as we go back into the school. I do not want to see the spot where my desk might not be. I stand outside the classroom until my teacher comes and tells me to come inside or I'll miss the assignment.

"Taylor, I'm trying to count to five while you hurry back to your seat," says Mr. Lock.

“One two three four five,” I say. I am proud that I have helped him count. Soon I am sitting in the office but everything is okay. I got a glimpse of my row when we passed the doorway of the classroom and my desk was still in it.

There is an aquarium at the back of the grade one classroom and inside are Painted Lady butterflies. The aquarium used to have fish in it, but they all died one weekend when the power went out. We have hatched the butterflies from eggs that turned into larvae, and now we are getting ready to let them go. Mr. Lock places the aquarium on a wheeled cart, and then we line up and follow him out of the school to the front sidewalk. When he lifts the lid, most of the butterflies use their wings to escape. Some of them can’t fly yet; their wings and bodies are too heavy for their legs, so they wobble when they walk. Mr Lock gathers them up and puts them on the peonies that grow beside the sidewalk and tells us they’ll be fine.

We look into the sky until all the other butterflies are gone and some of the kids chase them but I keep looking back at the ones on the peonies. I feel tears on my cheeks. Then we go back into the school. I don’t know why we hatched them if we were just going to let them go. There are a lot of birds in this world that eat butterflies. And the peonies are bright and dangerous-looking; I have never seen butterflies sitting on them by choice.

My Eighth Birthday

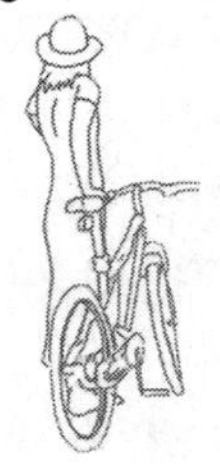

I am remembering my eighth birthday, December 27, 1991. I am remembering how I was having an interesting time sorting things in my room so that, when the doorbell rang, I didn't want to answer it. This is how my memories come to me, as if I am running a film inside my head and seeing everything happening again.

"Taylor, your guests are here," I remember my mother calling. "Open the door!"

How does she know who is on the doorstep? This is one of the mysteries I encounter in my childhood. My mother seems to know so much while I know so little.

I just keep sorting things in my room and when my mother answers the door, it is some of the girls from my grade two class, as she predicted.

"Taylor, come and play with your friends," calls my father. "I think they have gifts for you."

Gifts are unpleasant things if they are wrapped up. The trouble is that when someone gives you a present in a wrapped box, you don't know what is actually in there. The only wrapped presents I like are presents I have put into the boxes myself, but I have learned to pretend to like other people's presents because that is part of being an adult.

I go downstairs and see four girls. My mother made me invite the thirteen girls from my grade because that was the way to avoid anyone having hurt feelings. Four have come, and all four of them are wearing dresses. I do not know the names of these girls but I reach out and take their presents.

"Thank you," I say to each one.

"You're welcome," each says back.

In France when people say thank you, "merci," the correct response is "de rien," it's nothing. It seems every country has its familiar script for this exchange.

The girls and I drink grape Kool-Aid and then we play Spin the Bottle. My mother says, "This person will be the wealthiest," and she spins the bottle in the center of the circle where we all sit. When the bottle stops spinning, it points at one of the girls and then this girl giggles. Then it is her turn to spin the bottle. "This person will get married first," she says. The bottle stops at my mother. I don't know why everyone laughs—it's obvious that my mother will be married first because she *is* married. This is the dumbest game I have ever played and I want to go back upstairs to my room.

Next we play The Toothpick Game. We each get ten toothpicks and then we are supposed to walk around and talk to each other. If we say the word "yes," then we have to give a toothpick to the person we spoke to. The best way to do well in this game is not to talk at all and so I don't. I know that I won't win, but I won't be last either. When my mother rings the bell we count our toothpicks. I have ten. I come in second. Then I count the girls and there are still four. Nine have not come to the party. Maybe they were invited to other parties today.

After this we play Find the Button. My mother tells one of the girls to leave the room and then we hide the button in another girl's hands. I have never played this game before and at first I think it sounds like fun, but when the Finder comes back in and we chant, "Button, button, who's got the button?" I am surprised that she does not know where the button is. It's obvious. We gave it to the girl in the yellow dress.

"The girl in the yellow dress has it!" I say.

"Taylor, you're not supposed to tell!" cries my mother. "That stops your friend from guessing!"

We try another round. Another girl goes out of the room and we hide the button under the girl sitting on my right. When the Finder comes back into the room, we chant again, "Button, button, who's got the button?" I can't believe that the Finder does not know where the button is. These girls are all very dumb.

"Does Marcy have it?" she asks.

"No!" I yell, and give the girl next to me a little shove. "It's under this one's butt, stupid!"

"Taylor, you're spoiling the fun!" says my mother. She has a configuration of wrinkles on her forehead that looks just like an H.

"I don't want to play," I say. "These games are dumb."

“Taylor, mind your manners,” says my father, who has not been playing the games so he does not know that they are dumb games.

“Anyone who likes these games is dumb,” I say. “And I’m not playing anymore.”

“You sit there and be nice!” says my mother. Her voice is loud and it makes me stand up and kick the nearest thing—which happens to be the bottom of the girl next to me and I dislodge her bottom off the button.

“Bottom off the button,” I say. “Bottom off the button.” Soon everything goes white and then I am back in my bedroom where I wanted to be. I bounce on my bed. “Bottom off the button,” I say, over and over, and the words make a kind of nest for my mind to rest in.

I have often thought about this birthday and how things were afterward, because that was the night my father left. It’s just like a character said in Harold Pinter’s play, *The Birthday Party*: “Sometimes when people go away, they don’t come back.” Harold Pinter the playwright, not Harold Pinter who is my gerbil and who is at Shauna’s, in his cage, probably chewing himself a nest out of a paper towel tube that he will share with Samuel Beckett.

What Happened After My Eighth Birthday Party

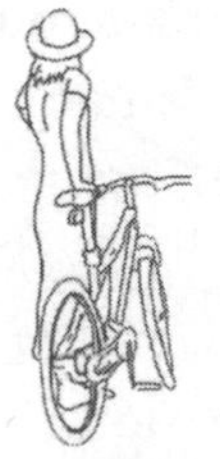

Eleven years have passed since the day my dad left. I turned nineteen on my last birthday, and I was glad not to have a birthday party. I have not had a birthday party since I was eight, and I am happy about that. I do not like birthday parties, just like Stanley did not like birthday parties in Harold Pinter's play, *The Birthday Party*. Party games frightened Stanley, while they disgusted me, so we have a slightly different perspective about this. But Stanley said he preferred to go out quietly on his own to celebrate, which is exactly how I feel about it.

"None of those girls are my friends," I told my father when he came to get me out of my bedroom for the second time the day of my eighth birthday. Dad talked softly to me, bending down so he could see me under the bed. Then he got loud and he started pulling on my legs. Dad finally dragged me downstairs and I was kicking and screaming.

"Here comes *The Freaker*," I heard one girl whisper. That

was the name they called me at school and I hated it. Hearing the name at home made me feel hot all over.

Somehow my father got me seated at the table. I did not eat anything and as soon as my father took his chair away from behind my chair, I fled back to my room. Everyone else ate the pancakes and syrup my mother had cooked, and pretended to have a good time without me. Or maybe they really did have a good time. I do not have any way of knowing for sure because of our different perspectives.

After the party was over, my parents had the last terrible fight and Dad left.

After my father left, my mother threw his things out their bedroom window. “And don’t come back!” she yelled. Standing at the window of my own room, I saw his clothes tumbling down from the house and I felt as if I were going to throw up. Suit jackets. Shirts. Pants. Suspenders. Clothes are meant to be in closets, not sailing through the air and landing on snow.

At that point, I forgot that my father had already left and I began to think that soon he himself would be flung out the window to follow his clothes. “Stop,” I squeaked, fear shrinking my voice. “Stop. The snow isn’t deep enough. The snow isn’t deep enough!”

But the falling things continued. I stood helplessly watching the garments settle, one on top of the other, on the crust of snow. It occurred to me that the clothes would get wrinkled, and then driven over when the car came out of the garage, and I wished somebody would pick them up, but I couldn’t move. Finally, I shook out my stiff body and crept away from the window.

My mother even threw a photo album. I don't know why. Later I saw that photo album in the basement, before she burned up all the pictures in it. In the pictures, my mother had on a wedding dress and my father wore a suit. There were no pictures in the album of my dead brother Ashton—and no pictures of me.

I wonder what would have happened if the kid in the blue sweater had come to my party. When the other kids called me *The Freaker*, would that kid have said, "Her name is Taylor Jane, and she is my friend"?

Anyway, probably the blue sweater wouldn't have fit by then and so the kid wouldn't have been wearing it. I had grown out of all my grade one clothes by the time I was in grade two. Good thing I am not growing anymore or I would grow out of my jean dress and then I would not be able to wear it anymore.

If I had that blue sweater I would put it in a picture frame and hang it on our wall at home. Here in France, there are a lot of interesting things on the walls. There are pictures of naked Egyptians. There is a cloth embroidered with a church on the front. There is a watercolor painting that I really like of the village of Lourmarin. The colors look as if they were put there in layers, which must have taken the artist a great deal of planning.

Why Seven is My Favorite Number

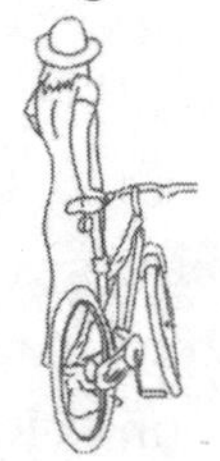

For a long time after my eighth birthday, I wished I were still seven. Last winter, when I met with the psychiatrist every week, she said I had a non-intrusive obsession with the number seven and she encouraged me to think about why I might have started to fixate on this number. I am rolling back this memory now, seeing our conversation as if it were happening again.

"Perhaps by looking for sevens, you are really looking for a way back to that happy time before you were eight and your parents still lived together," the psychiatrist says.

"Perhaps," I answer. "I never thought about it that way." I take another sip from my water bottle. I have the urge to take six more sips, but I stop myself. That's the thing about my obsession with sevens. I can control it, which means it doesn't control me.

"In the long run it will help you to know the contexts of

your obsessive behaviors," says the psychiatrist. "You can use calming strategies to help yourself in those contexts."

"I do not like to run," I say. "Let alone long distances."

"I mean, over a longer time period, you will be able to understand your obsessive thoughts better and have more control over them," she explains.

"I hope I can get control over them before my next job interview," I say. "Because I am getting tired of working only two hours a day at the bookstore."

"What are your goals for a job, Taylor?" asks the doctor.

"Well, maybe seven hours. That would be good," I say. "But just on some days, because on other days I will be taking university classes."

"You want to work in a bookstore?" she asks.

"Yes."

"You don't want to work anywhere else?"

"No," I say. And then I stop to consider. At that time I had only worked in bookstores, and so working somewhere else had never occurred to me. "Upon reconsidering, I have a different answer," I say. "I might like another kind of job, especially if it lasts more than two hours a day. You can't support yourself and be independent if you only work two hours a day."

This was a good answer, because if I hadn't wanted to work anywhere but a bookstore, I would not have this job in France. Many people would like to go to France and I am proud that Alan Phoenix trusted me enough to ask me to look after his son. He is paying me the Saskatchewan minimum wage for the mornings I am working, which is $7.95 per hour. When you add airfare and living expenses on top of that, I am making $2,322.50 per month more than I was making working part-time at the bookstore in Saskatoon. Since we are here for July and August, I will have made more than I would make at the bookstore in a whole year. And a job as a personal care assistant in France will look very smart on my resumé.

When Alan Phoenix told me that he had received funding to collaborate on a project with a well-known painter in France, and asked if I would come along to babysit Martin Phoenix, I was happy to accept the job. To my surprise, my mother agreed very quickly. In fact, not only did she agree, she said she would come, too. She said it was about time she got to see the world, and that now, thanks to Grandma dying and leaving her money in the will, she intended to get out and do things.

My mother and Alan Phoenix are drinking a lot at the wine caves but she does not sit around in her bathrobe, which is a change for her and a relief for me. If my mother had sat around in her bathrobe much longer last spring, I was going to give her my next appointment with the psychiatrist. Being obsessed with your bathrobe is probably the worst obsession a person could have because you can't go to work when you're not wearing the proper clothes. And if you can't go to work, you can't be independent. Luckily they hired a temporary secretary in her place while she is away this summer, or she would be fired for sure.

I am glad to be here in France putting "personal care assistant" on my resumé. It's surprising that almost five weeks have passed since our arrival on July 5. Just as surprising is that we only have three more weeks to go. I will be back in Saskatoon in time for university to start, which is a good thing.

An Afternoon that Begins With a Wine Cave and Ends With a Mail Truck

It is another rainy day and this is unusual for the south of France. Alan Phoenix says that Madame Colombe told him that this is the wettest year in thirty years. Usually, the grass here is dry and there are bald patches. But now the ground is covered with vegetation and even the mountains are green all over.

Yesterday afternoon I went with my mother to a wine cave where she tasted eight different wines but did not get drunk. I tasted some wines too and they all tasted like fish. Beside the wine cave was a wine museum, started by the great-grandfather of the man who owns the wine cave, and my mother paid ten euros for each of us to go through and see the wine-making artifacts. The temperature in the museum was a pleasant 19 degrees Celsius, according to an old thermometer on the wall, and there were six rooms painted beige. One of the rooms contained old equipment for cutting the vines and I hadn't realized how many different varieties of scythes and sickles there were for slicing the stalks by hand. Another room contained the presses that squeezed the grapes into juice. I found out what makes the different colors of wine: it's the skins of the grapes. The red skins are left in the mix for only a short time to make rosé wine, but left for a longer time to make the red wine.

The presses had big tubs with lids slightly smaller in diameter than the tubs themselves; these lids hung over the tubs on wooden nuts and bolts. By swinging a lid, you could force it down tighter and tighter onto the grapes. This would feel very comforting if you were a person sitting inside the tub and if the pressure was just right. If it were built correctly as a "human press," I could control the pressure by manipulating the lid to come down on top of me as I sat curled up in a tight ball. For me, that would replace things like rolling up in sheets and squeezing under furniture for the calming effects deep pressure offers. I wonder if anyone has ever made a human press.

One of the rooms was full of bottles and the oldest ones had no seams because they were blown by hand. You could see that these bottles weren't a regular shape due to human error. The bottoms rose up a long way inside most of the bottles; this makes you think you are getting more wine than you actually are. There were also bottles shaped like animals and people. There was even a bottle made to resemble a Canadian Mountie. This was the only reference to Canada in the museum. It is strange that, since I have been in France, this is the only thing I have seen that represents Canada. It is interesting to me how a place as big and complex as Canada can be reduced to one thing: Mounted Police.

It was a pleasant afternoon, except that my mother was in it. She kept telling me to look at things I didn't care about and she distracted me from what I was really interested in. I wanted to spend more time looking at those wine presses. I thought about coming back to the wine museum on my own, except I'm not sure how I could get here.

"Maybe you would like to take a cooking course that teaches how to match wines to the food you eat?" my mother asked. "I could sign you up for one in Lourmarin. That kind of knowledge would be very useful."

"I am not going to take a cooking course," I told my mother. "I am going to work for the summer as a personal care assistant and then I am going back to university in the fall where I will be taking more biology classes."

"We'll see," said my mother. "It's important to be practical, Taylor."

As soon as I think about this conversation, I start feeling as trapped as if I were Stanley in Harold Pinter's play. Maybe I am just like Stanley, even though I wish I wasn't. Maybe when I get back to Saskatoon there will be a list of students for a cooking course—and my name will be on it. I cross my arms, pinch my earlobes, and do the deep knee bends my psychiatrist showed me as a calming strategy. Quite possibly I should use this strategy before talking to my mother, but that would mean doing it all the time and this would be very disruptive.

I wonder when my mother started making me anxious, instead of making me calm. When I was little and she was in my classroom, sitting on a chair with her flowered handbag on the floor, I felt happy and relieved that she was there. She doesn't make me feel happy and relieved any more. This might be the difference between an island of stability and a prison.

Martin Phoenix still has his rash. The doctor said that his rash was something called Pityriasis Versicolor. She said it would eventually cover his whole body and then go away, and that it wasn't contagious. Alan Phoenix said that this was ridiculous and that it was just diaper rash, but you cannot buy the creams here without a prescription and the doctor wouldn't issue one. Luke Phoenix said that the consultation was an easy way for the doctor to make twenty-seven euros.

My mother said to shake some cornstarch onto the rash, because that is what she had successfully used with me when I was little and I had diaper rash. It is embarrassing when my mother talks about this. I would prefer that my friend and potential brother Luke Phoenix not know about my diaper rash as a baby. People's childhood rashes should be private.

"That is a private thing," I told my mother when she started talking about my diaper rash.

"Never mind," she said.

Martin Phoenix used his Tango to say that the doctor was hot and could he go back there tomorrow. Alan Phoenix laughed at him and said the doctor was too old for him, although she is probably rich and might be helpful around the house. Martin Phoenix said that age and money aren't a factor if you're really in love.

"Just beauty," said Alan Phoenix, and kissed my mother on the cheek. I looked the other way. They'd just better not get married this summer or this personal care assistant job won't count. It has to count or I can't put it on my resumé. And if it's not on my resumé, there will be an empty space representing this summer—and empty spaces do not look good to prospective employers.

"Over and under," is the phrase that irrationally sings in my brain. "Over and under, over and under." I sing it seven times, and then I stop.

From my window as I type this journal onto my laptop, I can see the yellow mail truck turning into the lane. I avert my head or I know I will sneeze because of the yellow. I listen carefully to the neighborhood sounds. There are different barking noises depending on the progress of the truck. At the beginning of the lane, there is deep, chesty barking. Next there is short, sharp, high-pitched yipping. After that I hear growling and snapping—this is from the big black dog that they keep on a chain in the yard. When somebody passes, it runs toward the fence where it is brought up short on the end of the chain. Finally there are many barking sounds at once, because the last house has five dogs. When these five dogs bark, the first ones start up again, but by the time the truck gets to our driveway, which is a long one banked by olive trees, the barking has stopped. I have not seen any cats along this street. I like cats but I do not like dogs. It's not that I'm afraid of dogs. I don't like them because of their smell and their barking.

I wonder if barking is an obsession, like cleaning was for

me before I went on medication for Obsessive Compulsive Disorder and worked with the psychiatrist on self-management. Maybe there is medication and therapy for dogs, but I doubt it. I still want to clean sometimes when I'm feeling anxious, but I can usually talk myself out of it. And when I am in my rage circuit, I mostly just swear inside my head, not in the open. I put my anger in the soles of my feet, where it can't hurt anyone, like my psychiatrist taught me to do.

The mail truck drives right up to our door. I watch as a man in a uniform rings our doorbell. Alan Phoenix is in his studio and might not hear the bell. My mother has taken our rented car to the Hyper U to buy chocolate-filled croissants because we are out of them, and that's all people seem to want for breakfast these days. Luke Phoenix has taken Martin Phoenix on a walk to Vaugines, where they both wanted to see how much fun it was to go down the hilly streets with the wheelchair, even though they both had to wear their raincoats and my mother said Martin Phoenix had to wear his bike helmet and that both of them should watch out for cars.

I wait for a minute to see whether Alan Phoenix will hear the doorbell after all. He does not, so I go down to the front door.

I dislike opening doors to strangers because these are people I do not know and anything could happen. I am like Stanley in the play when Stanley confessed to being afraid of a van coming with a wheelbarrow in it. When I was little I was especially afraid of delivery vans. Today I know that when I open the door, the yellow mail truck will be in the street and I will try not to look at it. But when I open the door, I do look at it—I can't help it. Then I sneeze.

"A vos souhaits," says the man.

"Merci," I say. "Parlez-vous anglais?"

"A small bit," says the man. "I have package for Taylor Jane Simon. Is she in the house?"

"That is me," I say.

"Sign on the ending," says the man, holding out a clipboard on which is fastened a piece of paper. There are many different colors of ink on the paper, and some things that I think are called logos.

"Where did this come from?" I ask.

"J'ne sais pas," says the man. "Sign on the ending. Your name. On the line."

"But what is inside?" I say.

"Open and see," he answers. "Ouvrez." He gets back into the van and I try not to look at the vehicle, but I do look and then I sneeze again.

I put the big envelope on the table. There could be good news inside, but there could be bad news. Or it could be a mistake and something not meant for me at all. Or someone mailing a poisonous substance—I've heard about people doing that. Part of me wants to open the envelope and part of me doesn't want to open it. I can hear the dogs barking together all down the lane.

The envelope is covered with French writing. I don't know anyone in France. Who could have sent me this? I move the envelope from the table to the buffet and from the buffet to the coffee table, where I put a pile of art books on top of it. Then I go and wash my hands. This is not part of my OCD, it is just being smart because of the germs that could be inside that mail truck with all the fingerprints it has collected during all the time it has been in operation.

The Mysterious Envelope

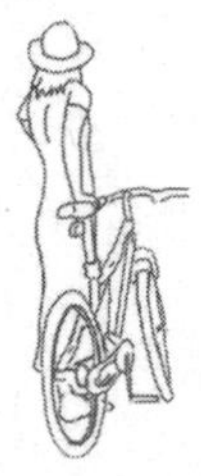

It is the same day as before and I have been sitting in my room and thinking about the envelope. I still can't decide what to do. My eyes burn. I am tired today because I woke up last night and could not get back to sleep. I kept thinking of all the French words I had learned and then of all the English words I wished I knew in French, and then I repeated an hour of English-only vocabulary in a French accent. This got me very awake. I opened my bedroom window as well as the wooden shutters that we close at night and leaned out to breathe the smell that is lavender from the fields nearby. I could see the yard from the light that we leave on atop the garage, and bright bats flitted back and forth. I could see the tops of the Luberon mountains against the sky, and then stars. The Big Dipper was facing me, with its handle to the left, and sometimes it looked as if the bats were being tipped out of it.

I knew that someone else in the house wasn't sleeping either, because somewhere in the house a radio was broadcasting the *Nostalgique* station that plays both French and English songs. We hear it driving in the car because it is Alan Phoenix's favorite; Martin Phoenix calls it Nostril Cheese, I don't know why. As I watched the bats, someone on the radio was singing, "I don't know how I could have dreamed a night like this," which I thought was very appropriate.

Now I can hear the rooster screaming from somewhere down the lane and, every now and then, a cuckoo. I count the repetitions of the cuckoo's call, and it is seven. I count the repeated units in the next call. Seven. And in the call after that: seven. I wonder if the cuckoo has OCD.

As long as I do not open the envelope, nothing has changed. Once I open the envelope, any number of things could change. Maybe it's better not to open it.

Beginning With a Dream and Ending With a Letter

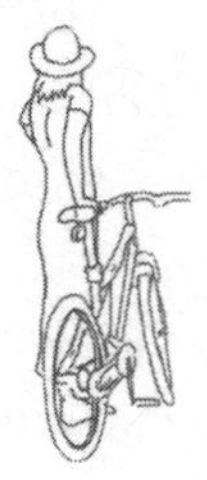

After thinking about the envelope for a very long time this afternoon, I must have slept for a while. I dreamed I was in the woods carrying the white bicycle. The dream was almost exactly how it had happened in real life. In the dream I was following the red-and-white trail, marked with stripes of paint on the trees, and it led me into the forest on a path that went from gravel to dirt. There were tree roots and rocks that made the path difficult so I began to carry the white bicycle. The path descended through an old stream bed and then up and around huge tree roots that I struggled to navigate. Rocks were strewn along the way, and I kept stumbling, but going forward. This part of the dream was just like how it happened when I went into the woods for the first time with the white bicycle.

In this dream, though, I kept hearing my mother calling

me. This isn't what happened in real life but could very well have happened—because, wherever I go, my mother is always demanding that I do this, don't do that, do this, don't do that. In fact, my mother is a pest. In my dream, when she called me, I tried to escape from her by heading deeper and deeper into the woods.

Heat from the sun fell through the thin leaves of the olive trees and my skin hurt. The cicadas were singing their electric song. Off to the left, I passed an older couple, one of them sitting on a fallen log in the shade, the other standing in a ray of light. Now my dream was back to how it really happened when I was in the woods that first time.

"Bonjour," I said. The one standing nodded.

"Bonjour."

They seem to be waiting for someone, I thought, but I knew they weren't waiting for Godot like the people in Samuel Beckett's play. Sometimes, I feel like I am waiting like that and I don't know what I'm waiting for, and it's not a nice feeling. It's a panicky feeling. It's a feeling that makes me want to swear and clean things, just like I'm trying not to do.

After I said hello to the people, I carried the white bicycle past them and kept going forward into the woods, and the path grew more and more difficult. Scaling a sharp ridge I fell and scraped my shin, and then finally I came to a stop.

Go back. That was the best choice. I toiled through the white haze that clouded my vision and started back, sweat dripping down the back of my neck. This time the couple were both in the shade, one still on the log, the other stretched out on the ground. I took a deep breath and the haze cleared.

"Bonjour," I said, my voice cracking. "Bonjour," I repeated.

They did not answer in the dream, just as they had not answered me in real life. I felt them looking at me, judging me, just like most of the other kids judged me when I was little. I wished I could climb out of my skin and be somewhere else. The heat was terrible, and in the end I wasn't sure I was on the same path as before. Even the stream bed, once I came to it, looked different. But I emerged from the forest and put the white bicycle down on the gravel road, slipped onto the seat, and put my feet to the pedals. Soon the wind was at my back and I skimmed along home, lost, and then found. C'est la vie; *such is life.*

Life is not a dream, but it can be the substance of dreams. And life can inspire dreams when you are awake as well as when you are asleep. In my sleep I dream of entering the forest with the white bicycle, but when I am awake I dream of other things. Self-understanding. Independence. I wonder how my dreams might be connected.

I slept until my mother came home. The first thing I saw when I opened my eyes was my mother looking at me. She wanted to see if I was awake and now I am. My mother is a pest—and she needs to learn that when somebody is sleeping, she should leave that person alone. Just because she is awake doesn't mean everybody has to be awake. We can all have our own perspectives.

It's strange how people can wake each other up by staring at them. I wonder about that sometimes. Eyes have a kind of power that I don't like. Looking at people's eyes makes me very uncomfortable, so I don't do it—except for sometimes when I remember that it is polite to make eye contact with a person when they are speaking. Mostly, I just look at people's eyebrows.

In addition to checking whether I was awake, my mother wanted to tell me all about going to the grocery store to look for cornstarch and how nothing was labelled clearly in France. I had to follow her down to the kitchen where she showed me the package. It was called "farine de maïs," and it did not have the picture of a rooster on it like we do in Canada. The French way makes sense—why would you have a rooster on a box of cornstarch? She also wanted to show me a bottle of wine.

"It's a sweet Bordeaux," she said, "and it only cost three euros! Imagine that!"

"I don't have to imagine it," I said. "I can see it right here."

The next thing I saw, after I saw the package of cornstarch and the bottle of wine, was the place where I had hidden the envelope. When my mother went out to the car to bring in more groceries, I went into the living room and pulled the envelope out from under the pile of art books. Still feeling the energy of riding the white bicycle in my dream, I tore open the sides of the envelope and pulled out the contents: a single sheet of white paper with delicate illustrations of lavender along the top.

Chère Mademoiselle Simon,

Merci d'avoir sauvé ma mère. Adelaide est à la maison aujourd'hui, et elle va aussi bien que possible, étant donné son âge et les circonstances.

Vous nous feriez plaisir en venant prendre l'apéritif ce

vendredi, 15 août, à 17h.

Meilleures salutations,

Francine Oberge

I studied the letter for six minutes and then I got out my laptop to help translate the words I was not sure of. When I was finished, this was what it said:

Dear Miss Simon,

Thank you for saving my mother. Adelaide is home now and as well as can be expected, given her age and the circumstances.

You would give us pleasure by coming to have aperitifs on Friday August 15 at 5 PM.

Best greetings,

Francine Oberge

I remember now: Adelaide is the name of the old, old woman at Cassis. I am glad to know she did not die and that she is back from the hospital. I will tell my mother to put Friday, August 15, 5 PM, on the calendar but I will not tell her now when she is banging around the kitchen. My mother seems to be in one of those moods she gets when she has PMS or menopause or both.

I wonder what temperature it is in the Oberge house and whether they have figs. I also wonder what aperitifs are. Are they supper? I hope they are not pigeon eggs.

Over the last few weeks, my mother has broken five wine glasses, and just now she broke a sixth. Perhaps she's the real *Freaker*, but I prefer to call people by their official names. My mother's full name is Penelope Simon and her initials are P.S. which may be why she always tries to have the last word in a conversation.

Learning to Draw

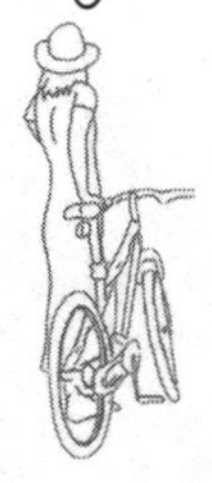

Sometimes I draw with the pencils Alan Phoenix has left with paper for Martin Phoenix and me to use. This afternoon I sat outside on a big rock, with one of the larger sheets of paper on an easel that was in one of the closets here, and I copied the scene in the painting that is on the wall of the villa. I wish I could stand where the artist stood, so I could do the drawing from real life instead of just copying someone else's work.

When Alan Phoenix saw my drawing he looked at it for a long time, rubbing the hair on the back of his head until it stuck up in wispy bunches.

"This is very good," he told me. "You should save it in your portfolio."

"I do not have a portfolio," I said. "What is that?"

"A collection of all your artwork. Start saving things, and I'll show some of them to Madame Colombe if you like."

"Why would your artist friend want to see my drawings?" I asked.

"She might have some advice for you," said Alan Phoenix. "For example, I suggest you keep working on these landscapes—and pay attention to the proportion of the things you are seeing. The buildings, for example. Are they really this size in comparison to each other? Learn to look."

"I don't know where to look," I said.

"Draw something around you," he advised. "And really look at it when you draw it. People need to learn to really look at things in order to draw them properly." I wonder if he really means that or if he means that people need to learn to see. I am looking and looking but it seems as if what I see is the variable in question.

Saturday, August 9

This afternoon it was too windy to draw outside and I sat looking through the window and thinking of the Painted Lady butterflies we hatched in Mr Lock's grade one classroom. What if they had been released here when they were too young for their wings to be strong? Would the wind have blown them all to pieces? I know that there are dangers here just as there were dangers for butterflies not ready to be free back home in Saskatoon. For example, I know that there are a lot of birds here, even though most of them are so secretive you hardly see them. Cuckoos. Sparrows. Magpies.

Seagulls, near the water at Cassis, are not so mysterious. Seagulls would have eaten up the butterflies in broad daylight if the butterflies had been released at Cassis.

When I think of butterflies I think of Adelaide, walking down to the sea in her butterfly nightgown. I was sitting on a bench in the shade of a big horse-chestnut tree in the middle of the town. I had been shopping and I was supposed to meet my mother and Alan Phoenix there at three o'clock. The street was busy and I kept seeing well-dressed women with shopping bags coming in and out of stores, and families with children clutching dripping ice creams, and men and women holding hands and kissing on the lips right there in the street. When two women met each other, they'd run up close and kiss each other on both cheeks. When two men met each other, they would do the same thing. I do not think this tradition is reserved for gay men; I think all men in France do this kissing.

There was a fruit stand and melons and peaches and other things were laid out for people to see and touch. People were tossing things into the air, and swinging bags of food, and reaching around each other to find what they wanted. I wondered if there were blueberries there but I didn't want to get lost in the busyness of the place. Everywhere things were moving fast. It made me dizzy.

And then the old woman appeared at the top of the street, walking down toward the sea. She was moving so slowly that I saw her right away amidst the fast pace of everyone else. I kept looking at her because it was easy on my eyes. One foot and then the other, shuffling forward—an old, old woman wearing a nightgown printed with butterflies. She wasn't carrying a purse and she wasn't wearing a hat. In this heat you are supposed to wear a hat. She was walking as if she wasn't used to it, as if she were a butterfly whose wings didn't work.

I stood up and followed her. I wanted to go up and tell her to put on a hat, but she didn't have a purse and I did not want to buy her a hat even though she should be wearing one. At the bottom of the street she turned left, toward the beach, and I kept following in spite of the fact that I do not like the beach.

The sand was gravelly and made crunching noises under my feet. People were lying on towels and sunbathing even though it causes cancer. They were lying so close together that it was difficult to walk between them, but the old woman found her way, and so did I. Some of the women didn't have any tops on and their private parts stuck out. I do not know if these were French women or tourists and I do not care. They would have looked better in tops no matter where they were from.

When the old woman got to the edge of the water, she kept going. The ocean got deep right away and the old woman's head went under the water.

I took the last few steps at a run and jumped in after her, even though I don't like water, especially water that has other people without tops in it and all kinds of fish and seaweed. I grabbed her around the middle and pulled her back to where she could stand up, my own feet slipping on the shifting sand. We stood there close to each other and I let go of her middle.

"Comment vous appelez-vous?" I asked.

"I don't speak French," she sputtered, water coming out of her mouth and falling down through the wrinkles. "Just English. I didn't know it would be so deep here. A hot day and people should be in water, but not over their heads."

"No," I said. "And they should have hats on."

She looked around. I don't know what she was looking at.

"And bathing suits," I said. She did not answer. I stepped back, out of the water and onto the shore, and she stumbled after me, clutching at my arm.

"What is your name?" I asked for the second time.

"Adelaide."

That is the part I forgot when I wanted to call the hospitals.

"I'm Taylor Jane Simon and my family and I are staying at the Le Colombier villa, near Lourmarin," I said. "Where do you live?"

The woman kept turning and looking all around and then she put her hand up to her heart.

"Hurts," she said, and grabbed onto me with her other hand.

A man nearby stood up and came over to us.

"Ça va bien?"

"I think she might be sick," I said, standing very still. He pulled a cell phone from his pocket and called a number. Two other people came over to us, and between them they got the old woman to lie down on one of the towels.

Soon an ambulance pulled into the street by the beach. The attendants brought a stretcher down to where we were and they lifted the woman onto it.

"What is her name?" they asked, but I had already forgotten it.

"What is your name?" they asked me. I wrote my name on a piece of paper, along with the name of where we are staying.

I wonder why Adelaide lives in France if she can't speak French. I also wonder what next Friday's aperitifs are going to be. I have looked up that word in the dictionary and it means alcoholic drinks or appetizers. If Adelaide's daughter serves pigeon eggs, I do not want to eat them. I have seen the pigeons here eating their own droppings. This could be a sign of a mineral deficiency or maybe they just don't know any better.

My Invitation to Adelaide's House

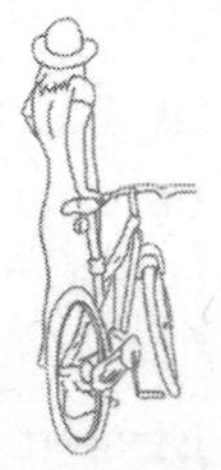

"I'm not driving you to Cassis and that's final," my mother says. It is Saturday evening and I have just told her about the letter.

"But I have been invited!" I say, and my voice is already in the red zone.

"Never mind. You can give that woman a phone call to ask about her mother, but we are not going there."

I feel a meltdown rising, along with my temperature.

"Why not?"

My mother answers but I can't tell what she is saying. The way her head is shaking makes me know she hasn't put an answer into the air after my question. I try to put the anger I'm feeling into the soles of my feet, but it's not working—the anger is too big to fit there.

"Walnut was the first of my series of gerbils!" I say, trying to hold onto the words before everything goes white. "After Walnut came June, and after June came Charlotte, and after Charlotte came Hammy. And last fall, before I turned nineteen, I got my fifth gerbil, Harold Pinter. Now Harold

Pinter is sharing the nest with Samuel Beckett and I hope neither of them is dead! "

As soon as I say this, I begin to worry that Harold Pinter is eating Samuel Beckett and I want to telephone Shauna, but my mother says it's too early in the morning there for me to call.

"The reason I should call is that if there is not enough fresh water or food in the tank, parent gerbils will consume their babies. Similarly, if there is not enough substance for nest building, or if the mother is stressed, or if Shauna or her husband touches Samuel Beckett and leaves their scent on him so that he is not recognized by Harold Pinter, it could be dangerous. *Gerbillus perpallidus*, the pallid gerbil, is part of the kingdom *Animalia*, the phylum *Chordata*, the class *Mammalia*, the order *Rodentia*, the superfamily *Muroidea*, the family *Muridae*, the subfamily *Gerbillinae*, and the genus *Gerbillus*. Due to their threat to native ecosystems, it is illegal to have gerbils as pets in California— and so we must never move there."

"Taylor, stop the gerbil talk!" says my mother. But I can't stop.

"And without adequate food and water, there can be serious health concerns in addition to cannibalism, including the eating of bedding material, stomach ulcers, dehydration, and starvation. It is conceivable that, if not cared for properly, Harold Pinter and Samuel Beckett could starve to death. What if their new environment causes epilepsy and they commence to have seizures?"

My mother starts to speak but I can't hear her. The silence pounds in my ears and it erases everything but my own hands, which I watch as they grip each other and don't let go.

When the world comes back into focus, I stumble up to my room and pick up Jean-Paul Sartre's little gray book. I reread my favorite passage, about how each person is in charge of their world and responsible for their situation. I think that is wrong. I am responsible for nothing. I am waiting for no one and responsible for nothing. These words circle around and around in my brain until all I hear is vowels.

When I start hearing consonants again I think about running all the way to Cassis but that wouldn't be a good idea. I have run away before, when we spent last summer at Waskesiu Lake, and all that happened is that I was late for my job the next morning. Running away was a bad choice then and it would be a bad choice now. Instead of running, I grab a cloth and start to scrub the desk in my room, and then I go on to scrub the walls. Obsessive cleaning is something I am trying to stop myself doing, so as soon as I can, I open my laptop and start to type. This makes use of my hands, but not all of my brain. *Sassafras. Iced tea. Chocolate pain.* ACEGIJL. Pi −3.141592653589793238462643383279502884197169399375105820974944592307816406286208998628034825342117067982148086513282306647093844609550582231725359408128481117450284102701938521105559644622948954930381964428810975665933446128475648233786783165271201909145648566923460348610454326648213393607260249141273724587006606315588174881520920962829254091715364367892590360011330530548820466521384146951941511

Controling My Anger

Last winter, the psychiatrist and I talked a lot about anger. We also talked a lot about my family and the things that made me anxious and mad. It's easy to replay our conversations, and I sometimes do that whether I want to or not. I wonder if everyone can see their lives like films replaying in their minds.

"We have been talking about your parents splitting up," the psychiatrist is saying to me. "Was it hard for you to adjust once your father left?"

"Yes," I say. "My father was the third person in our family, and without him, there were only two. It was hard to get used to that. Two is the smallest kind of family and I wanted back into the bigger one."

"I get the picture," says the doctor. Her name is Dr. Salmon but I do not like calling her that. She once told me I could call her Dr. S., but I do not like calling her that either.

I look around her office and I do not know what picture

she is talking about. Her walls are beige and bare except for a petit-point wall-hanging of a horse and its colt, and a framed picture of words with a blue-and-red crest at the top. I'm still not sure what she means about the picture but I don't remark on it. My mother has warned me that doctors aren't supposed to be interrogated, and I am trying not to interrogate this one. I also try not to look at her bookshelves. They are yellow.

"What bothered you the most about your father being gone?" she asks.

"The medicine cabinet," I say.

"The medicine cabinet?"

"You are just like the queen," I tell her.

"The queen?"

"The queen knows the way to keep a conversation going by repeating a few words of what the other person says. The queen knows how to do it. When she repeats a few words, the person knows that she is listening and keeps talking. Shauna taught me that."

"Shauna taught you that?"

"You are doing it again. Repeating the words. Shauna was the teacher associate who worked with me in school. She taught me a lot of things, like how to do a conversation and how to use the five w's in order to ask questions. She is married now and living in Edmonton but she and her husband are moving back to Saskatoon at the end of May. She has invited me to visit her when they get here."

"Taylor, what did you mean when you said the medicine cabinet was the thing that bothered you most about your dad's leaving?"

"His shelf was empty," I say. "And when one thing changes, everything changes. When I would get up in the morning and go into the bathroom to brush my teeth, I'd see that shelf and then I couldn't eat breakfast. Because I couldn't eat, my mother would send extra snacks to school with me, and the other kids would steal them. This made me so mad that I could not sit at my desk because it was near their desks, where they had hidden the food that they took from me, but it was not appropriate for me to look inside their desks, even if my food was in there."

I remember that time at school as if it were yesterday. It was not a happy time. Instead of sitting in my desk I would go and sit in an empty box that the teacher had left in the back of the classroom. It was because of my preference for sitting in the box and the yelling I often made in there that my teacher asked the school psychologist to come and see me. He referred me to a family psychologist, who prescribed medication. The medication made me feel outside of my own self in a bad way. I've heard that a lot of medications prescribed for children have never been tested on children. You can't be sure something is safe if it's never been tested. I felt somehow disengaged from my body.

I spent the rest of that year, and the next two years, unhappy and not wanting to go to school. For part of a school year I spent time in a class for kids with intellectual disabilities, where all the work was easy. Someone gave me play-dough to keep inside my desk, and to squeeze whenever I felt like it. I remember eating it, which might have been an effect of the drugs.

When I was in grade five, I had an appointment with a specialist who diagnosed me with autism, but my mother didn't tell me this until I was in grade six and back in a regular class. I think the school knew about my diagnosis because they let a woman called Janet help me with my work. That was a relief, except we spent a lot of time outside the classroom in a little room and I don't think I learned very much. I did a lot of coloring.

When I started grade six, I was introduced to Shauna—a new teacher associate assigned to help me translate emotions, which the specialist said my brain had difficulty handling. That's when my mother told me that my brain was different from most people's brains, and it was because of something called Asperger's Syndrome. Later, she asked me if I had told any of my classmates I had that. "No," I said. I mean, who would tell people about their ass burgers?

Shauna, the teacher associate, had me look at picture cards of people's faces, and we talked about the way the people were feeling. I learned to put a name to these emotions, and then, later, to my own. Once the emotions were labeled, I learned strategies to deal with them. When I was angry, I could take a break or ask for help. The school stopped sending me home because Shauna told them that this just taught me to melt down when I wanted to go home. I still had meltdowns from time to time but now there was a safe place I could go to relax, a little room off the supply room. Shauna said the meltdowns were caused by my emotions short-circuiting, and she told me to go to the little room before I melted down, as a preventative action. I wish there were little rooms like that everywhere. Now that I am nineteen I have other strategies when I get angry. It's just hard sometimes to use them.

In class, I still found it challenging to figure out what the teacher was saying if she was giving directions, but Shauna would sit with me and review what I was to do, and provide an example which I could follow. I started getting good marks on my report cards. And I stopped taking those drugs. Instead of taking the drugs, an occupational therapist told me to take walks around the school if I got agitated, which was about four or five times a day. At recess I ran around the track, and I ran again in gym class because I have an impossible time coordinating my body for sports so it was too hard for me to join in with basketball or volleyball.

To help me stay focused while I was sitting at my desk, I could chew gum whenever I wanted and I could drink water from a bottle with a straw to calm myself. Shauna told me that when I was in trouble, I just needed to think of a strategy. "Stop and think," she'd say. "What do you want to do to help yourself?"

I told all this to the psychiatrist last winter and she kept asking questions. She wanted to know if running made me feel calm. I told her that running does not make me feel calm if I am being chased by something, like a big dog. Or if I am in a contest chasing something, like a calf with a bow on its tail that I am supposed to pull off if I want to win a prize. It does make me feel calm if I am running for no reason, and afterward, when I sit down, I just listen to my breath and have no thoughts in my head.

The doctor taught me a couple of other calming strategies, such as deep pressure to the earlobes and a visualizing technique, where I learned to acknowledge my anger and then send it from my core down to the soles of my feet, where it's easier to manage. And she advised me to keep running on a regular basis, to take some of the stress out of my daily life.

"Could running take the stress out without taking anything else out?" I asked the doctor.

"Maybe you could try it and see," she said. And her mouth curved up. I think she was smiling.

Running might be a good strategy to deal with stress, but I don't think that running can help me now. Especially not running away.

Thinking of My Father

It is another rainy afternoon and I have been thinking of my father. Would my father let me go to Cassis if he were here? Probably he would drive me there himself because he doesn't think my mother is a very good driver. She only got her licence after he left home, and even she herself says that she is not a good driver.

If my mother marries Alan Phoenix, which I hope she does *not* do this summer, he will be called my stepfather, but Alan Phoenix does not have anything to do with steps, although there are steps up to his front door. I know there must be another reason why someone your mother marries is called a *step*father, but I do not know what that reason is. It would be strange to have both a father and a stepfather. Strange and useless. Nobody needs two fathers. Except if one will drive you someplace when the other cannot, because he lives in Cody, Wyoming, and you live in France. When I hear

Alan Phoenix come home I have a question I want to ask him about the driving.

My father looks like the singer Cat Stevens, with thick dark curly hair. Alan Phoenix has thin blond hair and does not look anything like Cat Stevens. I have visited my father twice since he moved to Cody, Wyoming. My mother talked about him moving to "the States," but it was really just one state and that is Wyoming. When he moved to Cody, Wyoming, he wrote me letters, but I did not like opening them and I did not want to write him back. He sometimes phoned to talk to me but I lost my voice whenever I tried to talk to him. It was uncomfortable talking to him when I couldn't see him.

Mom said we could go down to Wyoming for a visit, if I wanted to go, and that the ride would take twelve hours. She said she would stay in a hotel and I could stay at Dad's. She hoped Dad and I would work things out, whatever that meant.

It was a hard thing to decide. I had already filled up his shelf in the bathroom. I had eventually gotten used to the routine of everyday life without him. And I didn't want anything more to change. Then, for an early present for my twelfth birthday, Dad sent me a ticket to the Saturday, October 12, 1995 rodeo, and I knew suddenly that I wanted to go.

We arrived at midnight on Friday, October 11. We went to the door of Dad's new apartment. I was chewing gum like crazy, and I felt as if I was going to throw up. The door opened and there was Dad. He took a step forward and I took a step back. The walls were green. He lifted his hands. If I concentrate I can see the rest of it replaying in my memory.

"Don't hug me," I say. He lets his hands fall.

"It's good to see you," he says.

"Okay," I say. "Do you have an alarm clock?"

Mom puts my suitcase inside the door and then leaves. I follow Dad into the kitchen but I don't want to sit down. The chairs are yellow and I hate yellow. Suddenly I feel like sneezing.

"You look good, Taylor," he says.

"Thank you," I say. Shauna has taught me to say that when someone gives me a compliment.

"I don't have an alarm clock, just this clock on the wall," Dad says. "Will that be a problem?"

"No," I say. "I can manage with that." But this is a lie. I really wish there was an alarm clock here.

He looks at me for a minute, and I look at a chair. Then I sneeze.

"Do you want a drink of anything?" he asks.

"No. I should unpack," I say.

Dad shows me to my room and I go inside and close the door. It is weird, visiting Dad. After a while he calls through the door, "Come out when you like. I'm in the living room." I sit on the edge of the bed. Finally Dad says, "If anything's wrong, we can call your mother. She'll know what to do." I don't answer. In a while, I hear him on the phone. "She won't come out of her room or talk. I think you'd better come get her."

Mom comes in fifteen minutes and opens the door. She has her flowered bag over her shoulder. I am glad to see it.

"Time to come out," she says. I follow her to the living room.

"Transitions are hard," she says to Dad.

"I am very good in math," I say. "I have passed all the work in my grade. I know the way to add, subtract, multiply, and divide fractions, and I can change fractions into decimals. One third, for example, is .33 repeating. A repeating decimal means that it goes on forever. That's why we use fractions for measurement in baking, and not decimals, because it would be impossible to measure something for a recipe if there was a rule for that ingredient to go on forever. One of my favorite numbers represents pi. Would you like me to tell it to you?"

"Not right now," says Dad. He isn't smiling, so I can tell he isn't very happy. I can't think of anything that would make him happy.

"I don't want to sleep here," I say. "Is there an alarm clock in the motel, Mom?" She says there is and I ask if I can sleep there instead. She says I can and Dad asks if I still want to go to the rodeo tomorrow.

"That's what I came for," I say. He checks the time and says we'd all better get some sleep and then he asks what I would like to eat when Mom and I come back in the morning.

"Pancakes," I say.

"Still the same favorite foods," Dad says.

I had never been to a rodeo before. We got there early and climbed onto the grandstand before all the best seats were taken. The best seats are at the very top because then nobody's behind you. I sucked on the straw of my water bottle and tried to get used to the animal smells. Mom had prepared me by telling me all sorts of things about what the rodeo would be like. I knew there were going to be cowboys riding bucking broncos. I knew there was going to be cattle roping. I knew that there might even be a greased pig contest, where people try to catch a slippery pig. She was right—there were all these things.

When I went to visit my dad for the second time, last fall, I went to another rodeo. This makes two times that I have been to a rodeo with my father. I missed Canadian Thanksgiving during last fall's trip, and that was unsettling, but I met my father's girlfriend, Sadie, and that was good. If he marries her, then I will have a stepmother as well as a mother. I really think that one kind of mother is enough. I can see the benefits of having two fathers, if the second one can drive me places, but I cannot think of anything good about having two mothers.

At the second rodeo I went to with my father, the last event was bull riding. I watched as one of the bulls was forced into the pen below us. He was afraid, and I could see the whites of his eyes as he turned and tossed his head. Somebody had what looked like a straightened coat hanger, and was poking the bull in the sides through the wooden slats of the fence. I didn't like this and was just about to yell, "Stop!" when the gate opened and the bull came thrashing out, with a man in the saddle.

The bull was wild, bucking and twisting, with that rider on top. The man didn't last long, and was thrown off before the buzzer sounded. I was glad. The bull kept going and his sides were slick with sweat. Two horses and riders, and a dog, tried to corner him and get a rope on, but he crashed past them and streaked around the ring. His coat was gleaming, and I saw his belly heave in and out with each breath. It was terrible.

The bull finally ran out of the ring and into an adjoining pen, where the gate was shut behind him. Now that was a real freaker, I thought. My dad was smiling, and I was glad that seeing the bull had made my dad happy. I thought that people should not be allowed to beat up animals. The first time and the second time I saw this rodeo, I had such different feelings. This is something that makes me confused, because when I think back to my thoughts on rodeos, I can identify opposite reactions.

At the first rodeo, when I was almost twelve, there was a youth competition. I didn't understand exactly what it was all about, but Dad said something as he led me down the stairs about trying to pull the ribbon off the calf's tail. He said the winner would get a hundred dollars. I wanted that money, because I was too young to get a job and it was the amount of fifty weekly allowances, so I followed him. Before I knew it, I was in the ring with the other kids, and we were being given instructions by a cowboy with a starting pistol in his hand. There seemed to be no way out of the ring, and the gunshot nearly scared me to the death.

"Stop and think," I could hear Shauna saying, and in a few moments I decided I'd better run. I tried to get as far away from the other kids as I could. I saw the calf bolting in front of the kids, and I figured that they would chase it away from me, which was what I was hoping for. I headed in the opposite direction. Suddenly there was the calf. It had circled around and was coming straight toward me. As it brushed by, I saw the ribbon on its tail and because the bow looked so unnatural hanging there I reached out and pulled it off.

Dad was at the side of the ring, whooping and hollering. I ran over to him and he lifted me over the fence, and then the cowboy came riding up and handed me an envelope. I had won a hundred dollars. Dad was still smiling when we got back to the apartment, and he told Mom all about me being the fastest and smartest runner there.

I didn't tell him it had been an accident. I was glad we had made him happy, the calf and I. Mom and I went to the motel room. Then we went to bed and in the morning we packed up for home. I offered to pay for the rodeo ticket but Mom said Dad had covered it. I wonder what he covered it with.

Life is full of opposites. Adults think differently from children. When you are both the child and the adult, you can have different perspectives, even just within yourself. When I went to that rodeo last fall, it wasn't the same as the first time. Last fall my father wanted me to chase the calf again, and that made me mad. I am not a child who can play games like that. I am an adult who wants to go to university and keep a job. If I don't have a job I will not be independent and I will still be sharing a house with my mother when I am fifty. Each time I get an invitation, she will refuse to drive me there and I will have to stay in my room like Stanley in Harold Pinter's play.

Reading the little gray book by Jean-Paul Sartre that I found on my bookshelf here in France has taught me to think of myself in parts, and to be content with each part that I can comprehend, because they're all connected. My childhood. My adolescence. And now, adulthood. Stories that hold my identity run from past to present, carrying the emotions that I have at last learned to name correctly. Anger, and loss, and joy. Stories that together shape a life, my life, such as it is.

I am wondering what I should do about the invitation to Cassis, now that my mother has said I can't go. Stop and think, Shauna would say. Stop and think. But think about what? I do not know why we have different perspectives about the Cassis trip, my mother and I. Now that we are both adults, I would have guessed that we'd have the same perspective on more things, but this is not true. When I think about my mother, I see a picture in my head of the flowered handbag, and McIntosh apples, and a jar of Noxzema, and the pink quilt that we used to wrap ourselves in when we watched movies on Friday nights. These things do not help me understand her at all.

The last movie we watched together was on the airplane. My mother and I haven't watched movies at home for a long time. I don't know why.

Thinking About Cassis

How can I get to Cassis, without running away? I have been asking myself this question over and over and now it is Monday, August 11, at 4 PM. My mother won't drive me there. Alan Phoenix won't drive me there. I did not ask Luke Phoenix because the rented car has no insurance for him and so he does not drive it at all. I can't run there and I can't walk there.

Then suddenly the answer comes to me. I can take a bus. There is a bus stop at the end of our lane, and a schedule on the wall of the shelter. I can bike to the shelter, read the schedule, figure out the appropriate time to be there for the bus to Cassis, and then make a careful plan about what time I need to leave here if I am to be in Cassis for aperitifs. This is what a smart person would do if she wants to go to Cassis and her mother will not drive her.

"What's wrong with your toenail?" I can hear Alan Phoenix

asking my mother. They are in the living room and it is time I went down there and told them my plan. If I don't tell them, it is like running away—and I am finished with running away.

When I go down there, Alan Phoenix is sorting through the art books and my mother is sitting on the couch with wine glass in her hand.

"Don't ask," she says to him. I don't know why she would say that.

"It happened because of the pedicure," I remind her. I don't look at Alan Phoenix when I tell her this. He has not been very helpful about Cassis, and so I just look at my mother. She has not been helpful either, but because we are related I have to talk to her now and then.

"The damaged part caught inside my shoe today and part of it peeled off," she says to Alan Phoenix, after she inspects her foot. "Never mind. It'll be fine. That's why I've been sleeping with my socks on. Because I knew it would gross you out." To me she says, "You should try some of this supermarket Bordeaux. It's very good, and so cheap here!"

"Your toenail looks like pictures of toenail fungus I found on the Internet," I say.

"Never mind!" she says, and now her voice is in the red zone. I have noticed that on this trip the voice most often in the red zone is hers. "You could get busy around here and help out, Taylor, instead of not minding your own business."

I take a deep breath and say the thing that I have been practicing to myself. It is better than running away, and it is better than doing nothing.

"On Friday afternoon, I am going to Cassis. That is four days from now. I will go there on a bus and I will be back in the evening. I will be able to do my work with Martin in the morning, as usual."

There is a sharp intake of breath and I think it is my mother's.

"Don't be ridiculous. You can't just run off by yourself."

"I won't be by myself and I'm not running. I am going on a bus with other people. I know that there will be at least one other person on the bus and that is the bus driver."

"You cannot go there on your own, Taylor. Even if you got to Cassis, how would you find this old woman's house?"

"What's her name again?" asks Alan Phoenix. He has not been paying good attention. I told him her name yesterday when I asked him to drive me. When he refused to drive me he explained that he did not want to get between me and my mother. I do not understand what he meant by that.

"Adelaide. Her name is Adelaide. But it's ridiculous to go all that way for tea. Taylor can just give her a phone call."

"It's not tea. It's aperitifs," I say. "And as long as they are not pigeon eggs I will eat them."

"You're not going, Taylor, and that's final!" says my mother. She gets up from the couch and goes into the bedroom she shares with Alan Phoenix and slams the door. It is not good to slam doors; it is hard on the hinges. At least now her door is closed, so she will not be tempted to slam it again.

I hear the bang of the oven door.

"Suppertime!" calls Martin Phoenix with the voice from his Tango.

"Come and get it before we eat it all!" says Luke Phoenix, carrying a casserole dish outside through the patio doors.

"You shouldn't slam the oven door," I say. I also want to tell my mother not to slam doors, but she is having a meltdown in her bedroom and probably wouldn't hear me. If she learned to put her anger into the soles of her feet she would function better. I decide not to think about my trip to Cassis just now. Sometimes, it's better to not think about things all of the time when you can think about them only some of the time and be calmer.

I watch Luke Phoenix carry more food out to the table. Luke Phoenix isn't hot but he does have nice red hair that is curly and wispy around the back of his neck. He has stopped wearing corduroy pants and for the first time he is wearing shorts. His legs have a lot of hair sprouting out of them.

It suddenly occurs to me what my mother meant when she told me I should hang around with other young people. What she meant was that I should not collect Luke Phoenix as my next boyfriend. This is embarrassing advice. Luke Phoenix is my friend. He is not someone I think of in that other way. I am glad my mother is in the bedroom having a meltdown. I wish she would stay in there.

The table in the backyard has a lot of food on it. While I go out and count things, I hear Alan Phoenix going into the bedroom. First he closes their window, pulling in the shutters that open onto the table where we are going to have dinner. Then I hear quiet voices talking, but I can't hear what anyone is saying.

In a little while, he and my mother come out and sit at the table.

"You fellows have done a good job," says Alan Phoenix, waving his hands over the table. "What kind of meat is this?"

"Lapin," says Martin Phoenix, turning up the volume

on his Tango so it sounds as if he is announcing to a large audience.

We all look at the table. There are small bowls of salad. There is a casserole dish of macaroni and cheese. There is a plate of meat on its own bones. There are big bowls of croissants. I sit down and pick up a croissant. It is filled with chocolate.

"What is *lapin*?" asks my mother.

"Uh ... it's rabbit," says Alan Phoenix. "Is that what you boys got at the Vaugines market?"

"Yeah, lucky we got there before it shut down. They close at 1 PM, you know," says Luke Phoenix. "It was the last rabbit they had. There was this lady who had her eye on it, but we got there first."

"Rabbit?" repeats my mother.

"You didn't push into line with Martin's chair, did you?" asks Alan Phoenix, pushing his lips out into a puckered frown.

"His chair has to be somewhere," Luke Phoenix says.

"I don't want to hear about you using Martin's chair to your advantage," Alan Phoenix says. "That's wrong and sets him a bad example."

I try to listen but I take a bite of the croissant. It is delicious.

"Chocolate pain is the best," says Martin Phoenix with his Tango.

"It's not pronounced 'pain,'" says Alan Phoenix, laughing.

I take another bite of my croissant. I like it a lot.

"It's a pain to see it and not eat it," says Martin Phoenix and he makes his laughing sounds.

Luke Phoenix eats an olive and spits the pit at his brother.

When the pit hits Martin Phoenix in the head, Martin Phoenix wiggles and Luke Phoenix says, "Hot cross buns!" and Martin Phoenix uses his Tango to say, "You are a poop." I still don't understand why Luke Phoenix talks about buns. Could this be a script that just means "Gotcha?" People should just say what they mean.

I try a little of the sweet Bordeaux. It isn't bad. It isn't good, either, but at least it doesn't taste like fish. I am happy that it only cost three euros.

I decide to keep not thinking about my trip to Cassis right now. Sometimes, it's better to postpone thinking of things until later. What I do think about is my mother and me. *Who has responsibility for my existence?* I wonder. I remember Jean-Paul Sartre's little gray book and think: *How can I be free if I don't make any decisions for myself?*

I take another chocolaty bite. She can tell me not to go all she wants, but my mother isn't the boss of me. On Friday I am going to Cassis whether she likes it or not.

Tuesday, August 12

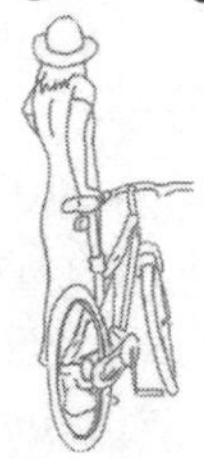

Today, I followed the schedule but my mother stayed in her bedroom with a headache. I do not know if she really had a headache or if she was just reading in there.

I am thinking about Friday and wondering if I really should take the bus to Cassis on my own. I want to make this decision but my mother is on the other side of the argument trying to force me to make the opposite decision.

Three more days until Friday.

Wednesday, August 13

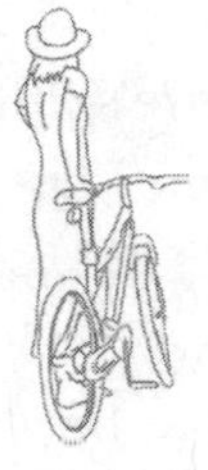

It is Wednesday, two days before I might take the 2 PM bus to Cassis. It is a cooler day and I have finished my work with Martin Phoenix. The little red circles have covered his whole body, just like the French doctor said they would. Pityriasis Versicolor. The cornstarch hasn't helped. Clearly my mother does not know everything.

The sky does not look as though it is going to rain, so I get the white bicycle and follow the red-and-white trail into the woods. I have been here before in real life and in dreams, but this time I am determined to get to the end of the path where there is a road, according to the map. If I do not find the road, I will not be able to go up the mountain and I think the view will be better from up there.

When the path becomes too rough, I carry the bicycle over rocks, an old stream bed, huge tree roots, and a sharp ridge. A downward turn and the trail is scattered with horse manure, which I navigate around. Martin Phoenix would like this, I think. I continue, and in six minutes I see what I have been looking for. A road.

The road winds around through vineyards and lavender fields. I stop when I see something glimmering in the ditch, and it is a broken mirror. It is a small one, maybe a rearview mirror from a motorbike. All the pieces are in the frame and it looks like some kind of puzzle. When I look into it, all I see are pieces of me.

I think of Jean-Paul Sartre's little book. Who am I? Am I someone, anyone, or no one? Last fall, when I read Samuel Beckett's play, *Waiting for Godot*, I thought about spending your life waiting. What if I was waiting for no one, and the no one was me? I don't want to be waiting for anyone, but the trouble is that I don't know whom to stop waiting for. I used to be waiting for boyfriends, but now I know that I don't need a boyfriend to be an adult. Then I waited for a job, but now I know that just having a job doesn't make you independent. I also know that it's hard to stop waiting when you don't have all the facts.

Near the broken mirror is a French cigarette package. Smoking is bad and whoever left this here is double bad—once for smoking, and once for littering. I take photographs of the cigarette pack, the broken mirror, and the red-and-white trail. These will be important pictures to store in the album that I will make to show other people the details of my trip. I can keep the images in my head, like frozen pictures or movies, but it's hard to show these to other people without a photo album. Photo albums are kind of like rearview mirrors for family and friends. They let people look behind you at things that have already happened.

When I pause on the hillside and look toward the village, I am surprised and pleased. I am looking at the scene in the painting on the wall of my bedroom. I stand for a long time and look. I try to really see what is there. At the same time, I am also seeing things that the painter missed. I see the view in layers just like the painter created in the watercolor, but I also see pieces that are missing. When I get back to the villa I will do a sketch of my own. It will show all of this and so I do not need to use any more words about it here.

As I turn back toward home, I see a different road connecting to the one I'm on. I discover that it leads closer to the villa than the trail through the woods, and I am glad to take it. One way carrying the white bicycle was enough. I am glad to be done for now with the forest.

"The woods are lovely, dark, and deep," I have heard Luke Phoenix quote from a poem by Robert Frost. "But I have promises to keep/and miles to go before I sleep/and miles to go before I sleep. Robert Frost, 1923." The woods here are not exactly lovely. They are just a place that you have to forge through in order to get somewhere else. I wonder if sometimes life is like that, with places you just have to get through in order to be anywhere at all.

Thursday, August 14

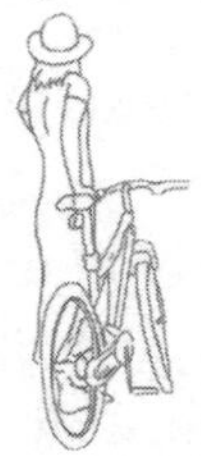

It is the night before I take the 2 PM bus to Cassis and my mother is still trying to convince me not to go. She has just left my bedroom in an angry mood and slammed the door. I have locked the door so that no one can slam it again. Slamming doors is very damaging to their hinges.

Before I came to my room, I helped Luke Phoenix and Martin Phoenix with the dishes. Martin Phoenix still has the ring rash all over his body. Pityriasis Versicolor. The French doctor was completely right and it is not diaper rash. My mother will have to think of something else to do with the cornstarch.

"'Do not go gentle into that good night,'" Luke Phoenix is singing from the hall. I think this is a line from a poem he has been studying.

"Is that William Shakespeare, 1609?" I ask.

"Nope, Dylan Thomas, 1951," he says, coming into my room and flopping down on the couch by the bookshelf.

"'Do not go gentle into that good night/Old age should burn and rage at close of day ... Rage, rage against the dying of the light.' Or something like that."

"What does it mean?" I ask.

"Don't give up without a fight," says Luke Phoenix.

"Are you talking about me taking the bus to Cassis?" I ask.

"I'm talking about life," he says. Then he stands up and heads over to the window. I look at his wispy red hair from the back and wish that he were my brother. But not until the summer is over and I have finished my job with Martin Phoenix.

"Are you waiting for someone?" I ask.

"You could say that," he answers, without turning around. "Or maybe I'm just trying not to fall off."

"Fall off what?"

"The world," he says, and laughs. I don't know what is funny until I remember that last year I told him that same thing when I was having a meltdown. You can get kind of dizzy when you're confused about something.

"I understand," I say.

"Well, join the club," he says, and laughs again but he doesn't sound happy.

"What kind of club?" I ask.

"It's just a saying," he says, and sighs. "Join the club—it means we are both sharing the same feeling."

"Okay," I say, and then when he doesn't answer, I say, "I get it. I get ..." I stop and then I remember something I have heard before. "I get the picture."

"No," he says. "No one gets it. No one really gets the picture, and that's the problem."

I know he is not talking about pictures. I go over and stand beside him.

"What are you talking about?" I ask.

"No one gets me," he says.

There are a lot of bright stars and this window seems to hold the whole sky. Down below, the yard light shines a pale yellow circle on the driveway. Suddenly I hear deep chesty barking coming from the end of the lane. Next comes the short, sharp, high-pitched yipping. Then there is the growling and snapping—the big black dog on its chain. Finally there are many barking sounds at once from the five dogs at the last house. When these five dogs bark, the first ones at the other end of the lane start up again, but in one minute and fifteen seconds all the barking stops. Then someone walks into the circle of light down below.

"Oh!" says Luke Phoenix. "Julian!"

"Who is that?" I ask, but he is already in the hallway heading for the stairs.

"Just a friend I met at the doctor's when we took Martin," Luke Phoenix calls, and then I see him outside, beside this Julian person, and then they are gone. I don't know where they went, but when I look outside all I see are the little bats, swooping between the cherry trees.

Later, when my mother comes back into my room, I am in bed pretending to be asleep. It is difficult to lie down with my eyes shut, but I force myself into stillness because the alternative is more fighting against each other.

"Tomorrow afternoon, we could visit a fortified village," says my mother. "It's close by and it's a shame to let all this history go to waste. And it would be a fun thing to do together. We could have ice cream afterward."

I do not answer. It is ridiculous to think of going to a fortified village when I might already be going on the 2 PM bus to Cassis and not be back until 9 or 10 PM. I do not know if my mother really wants to go to a fortified village with me, or if she is trying to find something to distract me from the idea of going to Cassis. It is exhausting to try and figure out what people mean with words that could represent any number of thoughts.

"Or you could take a cooking class," my mother goes on. "If you're bored, they're giving a cooking class at one of the local hotels. It's important to take advantage of things that are close by, Taylor, so that we make the most of our trip."

It's strange that my mother thinks of this as *our* trip, when it's really my trip. I found the trip first, and she basically invited herself along. Now she's trying to make the trip go all her way.

"I don't want to take a cooking class," I say, my eyes still squeezed shut. "Grandma kept telling me that I should study commercial cooking, but now she's dead and I don't expect to keep hearing about it from you. If you think a cooking class is so interesting, you should take one."

To Go or Not to Go

All Friday morning, I think about Cassis and change my mind from planning to go there today to deciding not to go there today. For the first two hours, Martin Phoenix makes science experiments and I clean up the messes we create. The best experiment is when we light a match and drop it into a glass bottle and then watch as the shelled hardboiled egg I place on top of the bottle gets sucked in with a loud gulping sound.

"It's all about atmosphere Rick pressure," says Martin Phoenix with his Tango. "That pushed the egg into the bottle."

"Atmosphere Rick. Oh, you mean atmospheric!" I say.

"You get the picture," he says.

"I do," I say. Then I ask, "Do you want me to program the Tango to say 'atmospheric'?"

"No," he says.

Martin Phoenix shakes a little bit and makes some sounds

and I know he is laughing. He is not laughing because something is funny, he is just proud of himself.

Luke Phoenix comes into the kitchen and pours himself a cup of coffee. It is 11 AM and he has missed his tennis lesson.

"Do you want to see an experiment?" Martin Phoenix asks.

"I am an experiment," says Luke Phoenix. I don't know what he means by that. He turns with his coffee cup and goes out of the kitchen.

"We are 233 meters above sea level here near Lourmarin," I say to Martin Phoenix. "And Saskatoon is 450 meters above sea level. Does this make a difference to the atmospheric pressure?"

"I don't know," says Martin Phoenix. "Google it."

We spend the rest of the morning using my laptop to search for details about atmospheric pressure. When it is lunchtime, Luke Phoenix doesn't come out of his room.

Alan Phoenix brings fresh bread, a new package of cheese, and some things that look like flaps of raw meat but which he says are honey ham. I eat some bread and cheese, and then my mother comes in, and she acts like she has PMS or menopause or both.

"Hammy lived to be four. Before Hammy I had Charlotte and before her I had June and before her I had Walnut and he was the first gerbil I ever had. And now I have Harold Pinter and Samuel Beckett but nobody will let me phone to see if they're okay," I say.

My mother looks at me and doesn't talk. I press my thumbs into my palms and tell myself that just because there's a cloth on the counter doesn't mean I have to use it. I get to my feet and there is a whirly feeling, but I take a deep breath and go up to my room. I think about what I need and put things into my bag. I think about how riding the bus will be familiar because I have ridden many buses before. I make sure I have the map I printed from the Internet, showing me how to get to Adelaide's house. When I go downstairs again, Martin Phoenix is in the living room.

"Have fun in Cast Seas," he says with his Tango.

"Martin, stay out of it," warns Alan Phoenix. I suddenly see now how somebody can get between two other people even if they're not actually standing in the way. I smile at Martin Phoenix.

My mother is doing the dishes and she does not turn around when I enter the kitchen. I feel my body shaking but I go right past her and out the door. I am nineteen years old and I should not be afraid of my mother, but I am. Stanley in Harold Pinter's play, *The Birthday Party,* is afraid of things he shouldn't be afraid of, too. But Stanley is stuck in his room eating cornflakes and I am not going to be like that.

People who are nineteen are not supposed to be afraid of their mothers. They are not supposed to be afraid of delivery vans or envelopes or packages. They are not supposed to be afraid of playground slides. I am afraid of all these things. I am also afraid of opening the door to strangers; however, this might be a positive thing as strangers could be bad. When I think about my future, other fears rise to consciousness. I am afraid of never getting a permanent full-time job. If I don't get a job, I will be living with my mother until she dies of old age. I used to be afraid of finishing high school, but I'm glad I graduated because you're not supposed to be in high school forever.

I think I know what happened to Stanley. Stanley is a person whose fears have beaten down his choices. More than anything, I am afraid of being like Stanley.

When I leave the house to go to the bus stop, I feel afraid of everything. My hands are sweating and I can feel sweat dripping down the back of my neck. When I go down the driveway and into the lane, and I hear the dogs start to bark, I want to run back to the villa and change my plans. But then I would never get to Cassis or talk to Adelaide or see what they are having for aperitifs.

An old man riding a bicycle turns into the lane ahead of me. From a distance he appears to be moving quickly, but as I get closer, I realize that, even though he pedals with vigor, in actuality the bicycle is barely moving.

Soon I pass the old man on the bicycle. Stanley would never have done this. He would have been afraid of passing anyone. I keep putting one foot in front of the other and when I get to the bus stop, I put some gum into my mouth. Peppermint, for calming and organizing.

I think Stanley has autism and he just doesn't know what to do about it.

Adelaide's House

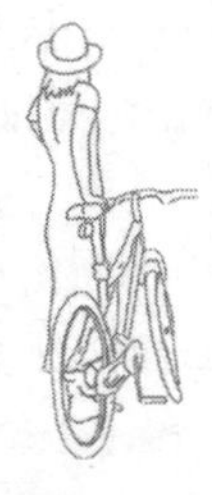

I arrive at Cassis at 4:30 PM. When I get off the bus, I look at my map and then start walking. Adelaide's house is not far from the bus stop and I can get there in half an hour, which means I won't be late.

It is a hot afternoon. I can hear the cicadas that are sitting in bunches of olive trees on the boulevards. They sound like an electric current, buzzing and buzzing. I pass an apple tree in someone's front yard and I think about picking an apple for my mother, but then I remember that I am mad at her. I walk across a parking lot and a lady comes up to me and presses a fig leaf into my hand.

"De l'argent pour les enfants," she says. *Money for the children.* I do not know what she is talking about. "Payé?" she says. I keep walking but she reaches out and makes the sign of the cross on my forehead. I jump back. She looks at me and then she grabs the fig leaf from my hand, turning away and muttering things in French that I cannot hear.

When I get to Adelaide's house, I walk up the front steps and ring the doorbell. A woman opens the door. She is wearing a light blue dress with white sleeves and she looks like my blue-and-white clock.

"Oui?" she says.

"Um ... hello, I'm Taylor Jane Simon," I say. "Is Adelaide here?"

"Pardon?" The woman looks at me with a blank expression. Then she repeats, "Taylor? Ah, oui! Vous êtes la jeune fille anglaise qui a sauvé ma mère!"

"Where is Adelaide?" I ask.

"Ne pouvez-vous pas parler français?" asks the woman. Then she says very slowly, "I am sorry. I speak very little English."

"Adelaide?" I ask.

"Lorsque vous n'avez pas répondu à l'invitation, je pensais que vous ne pouviez pas venir," she says, turning and walking down the hallway and then motioning for me to follow. "Please. Come in. We will sit in the living room."

"Is Adelaide your mother?" I ask.

"Oui, yes. I am Francine. Please sit down," she says, waving at the white couch. She herself sits on a sturdy leather chair near the doorway.

"I am here for aperitifs," I say, looking around. I do not see pigeon eggs. That is a good sign.

"Très bien, très bien," she says. I look around. On the walls are large paintings. They are all of the sea. One of them looks just like the beach at Cassis, with swimmers and sailboats nearer the shore, then bigger boats out in the expanse of ocean. The colors are brilliant, as if somehow light has been captured inside them, bringing the images to life.

"I like the paintings," I say.

"Très bien. Very good. All Adelaide's," says the woman. "My mother was a painter. She uses ... what is it ... acrylic wash."

"Was?" I ask. "Is—is Adelaide dead?"

"Ah, non!" laughs the woman. "Depuis qu'elle a eu son attaque..." she begins, "since she had her—her stroke—no more painting. No more painting since last year."

I rub my hands on the soft fur of the couch. The woman looks at me, and I look at her eyebrows. Silence hangs between us like a curtain.

"You don't eat pigeon eggs," I blurt, finally. I should not have said that. The woman looks startled. Or possibly constipated. It's hard to tell the difference.

"Pardon?" she asks.

"*Pigeon Eggs!*" I say. "I hope we are not eating them. For the aperitifs."

The woman jumps up.

"I will go—and get—Adelaide," she says. "Please—wait here."

"Fine," I say.

After a little while the woman—I forget her name—is back and behind her Adelaide shuffles into the room. She is wearing the butterfly nightgown. Adelaide's daughter says something I can't quite understand and then disappears to somewhere else in the house. Adelaide sits down beside me on the couch and runs her hands over the white fur covering.

"It's my birthday," she says rather inaudibly.

"What?" I ask.

"It's my birthday. Today is my birthday," she says.

"Well," I say.

"Aren't you going to say Happy Birthday? The rest of them have been saying it to me. All day I keep hearing it," she continues.

"Is it?" I ask.

"Is it what?"

"Is it a happy birthday?"

"No." she says. "I don't like birthdays. I've had quite a few of them. I've been having them since I was born, Saturday, July 25, 1908."

"You're 95 years old," I say.

She looks at me with milky blue eyes.

"Rather enough, don't you think?"

I look around the room. There is a fish tank on a stand against the wall. In it, angel fish hang as if suspended in the water.

"That's what they gave me this year," she says. "That tank and those fish. It's a strange kind of amusement. What kind of a life do they have in there?"

I say nothing and she goes on.

"They also gave me a new hat, a purse, three or four little doodads for my dresser, and a large cake that no one has eaten yet. People get far too many gifts these days. One gift would suffice. One would certainly suffice."

"We're not going to eat pigeon eggs, are we?" I ask.

"I certainly hope not," she says. "Disgusting things, pigeons. They eat a lot of shit, you know. Francine likes pigeon eggs, but then she likes anything French."

"Why ... how is it that you speak English and your daughter is French?" I ask.

"Good question. A very good question." Adelaide is breathing heavily now and she sits for a moment and catches her breath. "I was born and raised in Squirrel Hills, Saskatchewan. Nothing wrong with that. Became a teacher. Taught in one-room schoolhouses. Met a man and married him, came to France, had Francine, and then the goddamn bastard abandoned us here. The rest is history."

"History?" I ask.

"The sort of thing that goes on and on, no need to talk about it," she says.

We sit in silence until Francine comes back carrying a hanger. On the hanger is a blue dress the same color as her own.

"Viens te changer, m'aman," she says. I think she wants her mother to change out of the butterfly nightgown. Adelaide shakes her head and pushes the outfit away. Francine makes a strange sound with her mouth and then leaves the room. Adelaide and I sit in silence. In a few minutes, Francine comes back with a tray containing a pitcher and glasses which she puts on the piano bench.

"Du citron pressé?" she asks.

"No whisky?" says Adelaide.

"Taylor, would you—would you like anything to eat?" Francine continues.

"Aperitifs would be fine," I say.

Francine looks at me, then darts back out of the room.

"It's strange that you and your daughter don't speak the same language," I tell Adelaide.

"Yes," she answers.

I think about this. "My mother and I both speak English but we don't understand each other very well, either," I say.

"Have I met you before?" asks Adelaide.

"On the beach at Cassis," I say, remembering how she walked into the ocean.

"Oh. I wasn't born here, you know," she goes on.

"Squirrel Hills," I say, pouring some of the juice into a glass and drinking it.

"Do you know where that is?" she asks.

"In Saskatchewan. I'm from there too. From Saskatoon," I say.

"I used to have them all sitting in rows," she says. "And even when one of the little blighters spelled something incorrectly, I never used the strap. We had the Orange Home near there, lots of kids with no parents coming to school. Needed an extra dose of kindness, those ones."

"Oh," I say.

"Took care of each other, though, I remember. Two sisters, always holding hands at recess. You have to stick together if your parents are gone."

"Oh," I say again.

"One time I was riding home—we all rode horseback in those days—and one of the farm boys rode with me. Grade six, I think he was. I had a bad headache that day, and the students knew it. A migraine. Instead of turning off at his road, he went with me right to the gate of my farm. 'In case you might fall off,' he said. That was a real little gentleman."

I drink the rest of my juice—it tastes like lemonade—and pour myself another glass.

"A real gentleman," I say, repeating part of her statement.

"Not like that bastard husband," she says and I'm not sure if she is swearing or not.

"Left us here in France," she goes on, "with no way to get back. Do you like my paintings?"

"What?" I ask.

"My paintings. Do you like them?"

I look at the paintings on the walls.

"Are these all yours?" I ask. "All ten of them?"

"I used to have students here," she says. "We would work indoors—or outdoors when it was fine. They had to learn to look because that is something you don't learn in school."

"What?" I say.

"To paint. You have to learn to look," she says.

"Alan Phoenix told me that," I say. "He says in order to learn to draw you have to really look at something."

"Smart man," she says.

"But I think it's about seeing," I say. "You can look all you want, but if you don't really *see* what you're looking at then it won't help you paint it."

"Looking. Seeing. You can say it however you want, as long as you know what you're talking about. People from the north come here all year round for the sun. The light. Come and tour my studio."

"Francine said you haven't painted since your stroke," I say.

"She doesn't know," responds Adelaide. "She doesn't know everything."

We go carefully up the stairs and through a door that leads into a large airy room. I wonder why people have to learn to see and learn to listen. Why aren't we born knowing how to use the senses we have? I remember finding out that people learn to speak naturally, with the connections we already have in our brains, but in order to learn to read, the brain must reinvent itself. That is amazing.

At one side of the room a big window opens toward the ocean, and from here I can see the big ships, although they look tiny. This is how I am looking with my brain—really seeing—remembering that ships are actually big even though they look small right now. I wonder if Adelaide stared out this window before she left the house, that day she walked into the sea. Now Adelaide removes a cloth from the easel and shows me a sketch of clouds.

"I like clouds. They make an interesting subject," she says, looking out the window.

"Oh," I say. "Clouds make me uncomfortable because they are always changing. I try not to look at them much."

"To begin to draw is the first step," says Adelaide, picking up a piece of charcoal.

Suddenly, Francine is in the doorway.

"Oh, now Mother, que fais-tu ici ? J'ai des amuses-gueule pour toi et ta petite invitée, en bas dans le living-room."

"We're having a drawing lesson," Adelaide says, handing me the charcoal. "You try it."

I sit down on the stool and sketch in some of the shadows, thinking how the clouds would really look. These clouds don't bother me because they are only changing when I make them change by adding parts with the charcoal.

"Yes," says Adelaide. "Very good."

Francine makes a little noise and then I hear her high heels on the stairs. I wonder why she wears high heels in thc house.

"Nature is like a dictionary for artists," says Adelaide. "Not only in art but in life. Nature is a good teacher. It teaches us patience. To wait. Everything has to grow in heart and mind."

"I do not like waiting," I say.

"Waiting has its purpose," answers Adelaide. I do not understand some of this conversation.

She goes over and turns on a record player and soon there is music.

"Franz Liszt. A good choice for clouds, don't you think? I always draw or paint to music."

"Oh, you draw and paint to music," I repeat.

"My last exhibition was Mozart," she says. "I chose the music and illustrated passages, in watercolor. I always work with music. Classical. It opens the mind and it opens the heart."

I draw for a while and when I turn around, Adelaide is sitting on the couch with her eyes shut.

"Are you tired?" I ask.

She waves her arms. "Keep working. I am just listening to the Liszt." She pulls a patchwork quilt onto herself from the back of the couch.

Heels again on the stairs and Francine comes in.

"Je peux vous montrer le jardin," she says. "The ... garden? And then—Mother should have dinner soon."

"Stop interrupting my lesson," says Adelaide. "Go and find something else to do. Feed the fish, Francine."

"Francine wants to be the boss of you," I say. It's a pleasant idea in which a daughter bosses a mother. I think about this for a while.

"I am not driving you to Cassis and that's final," I say.

"But I have been invited!" my mother says and her voice is already in the red zone.

"Never mind. You can give that woman a phone call to ask about her mother, but we are not going there," I say.

"Why not?" says my mother.

I shake my head but I can't think of anything to say.

"Why not?" my mother says again, and knowing my mother, she will keep saying this until she gets an answer; that's how stubborn she is.

I take a quick look out the window and then I shade a few more of the clouds. Being the boss of my mother would take some practice, but I think I could get used to it.

"I know someone who hears only jazz. I could never work with jazz," says Adelaide.

I sketch a little longer.

"Art is liberty," she says.

When I turn around, her eyes are shut, and after a moment I hear a snuffling sound. Adelaide is sleeping with her mouth open. The patchwork quilt is pulled right up under her chin.

Adelaide's Garden

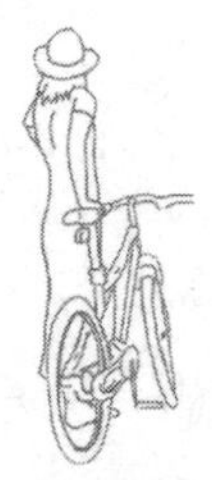

After supper, Adelaide pushes her plate away and asks if I'd like to see the garden.

"Mais, maman, tu n'as presque rien mangé!" says Francine.

"Okay," I say.

We go outside and it is like being in a painting with colors carefully planned and planted all around us. The flowerbeds are layered with pinks and purples and the trees are carefully placed to move a bystander's gaze from one grove to another.

"Those rose petals are edible," I say, remembering something my friend Paul told me last summer.

"Yes. When I was a child we used to bake them sprinkled with sugar. Those were the days when you didn't waste anything," says Adelaide. "My mother made pies from crackers when there weren't any apples. You could hardly taste the difference."

I nod because sometimes you can answer that way.

"Did you ever ride a bicycle?" I ask.

"Yes, I did. It was my brother's bicycle. There was a

sports day in town one Saturday and my father wouldn't drive me there. I wanted to do the high jump and he said jumping wasn't for girls. My mother packed me a lunch and I borrowed my brother's bike and rode the five miles to town. I had my period that day and wore a rag pinned to a garter belt, and I had cramps, but I entered the high jump. I ran at the stick and jumped by bending first one knee to the side and then the other because that's all I knew how to do. Other kids were doing fancy jumps, rolls and such, but I didn't know how. 'Look at that funny one jump,' a kid said when I was jumping. A man came up to me after the event and said if I learned a modern technique I could add six inches to my jump. I didn't know what he was talking about. I came in second, though. Even with my funny jump, I came in second. Then I biked home."

"Congratulations for coming in second," I say.

"When I got home, my father was setting out the pails to milk the cows. 'She's not milking the cows,' my mother said. 'Look at her face. She's just done in.' My mother sent me up to bed and my father didn't argue."

"That was nice your brother lent you his bicycle," I say. "I am borrowing a bicycle here. It is a white one and sometimes I ride but sometimes, when the trail gets hard, I have to carry it."

"I carry my age," says Adelaide, and I don't know what she is talking about. Then she says, "Most people carry something." She thinks for a moment. "Did we meet at Art School?"

"No," I say. "We met at the beach."

"Oh, yes," she says. "There was all that litter on the sand.

People today waste far too much. All these birthday gifts. When I was a girl, my father made me an elephant out of potatoes. He glued potatoes together and that was my Christmas present. And I treasured it. After it went rotten we put it on top of the frozen garden and then I had the space back on my dresser."

I nod again. A Pale Clouded Yellow butterfly lands on the front of Adelaide's butterfly nightgown.

Then Francine comes outside and the butterfly lifts away from Adelaide and disappears into the hollyhocks.

"It's almost Mama's bedtime," she calls. "Time to go—time for you to go home, Taylor."

Before I leave the house, Adelaide presses a card into my hand. When I'm on the bus, I read it. It is a doctor's appointment card, but she has scratched out the appointment details and written in the white space: *Come and visit next Friday.*

I think this means that Adelaide is my friend. Even though we are not the same age, we can be friends. My mother was wrong.

When I get home, it is very dark and I walk along the lane to our villa, listening to the crescendo of the barking dogs. As I go up the hill to the house, I see bats swooping in the yard light, and to my right the outline of the cherry trees. I am glad I am working in France this summer or I would never have seen these things.

There is somebody under one of the cherry trees and for a minute I feel afraid and stop walking.

"It's just us, Taylor," says a voice.

"Who is out there?" I ask.

"Me and Julian," says the voice, and now I recognize it as Luke Phoenix's.

"What are you doing under the cherry tree?" I ask.

I hear whispering voices and then two figures come toward me and, until they get close, I am not sure that one of them is Luke Phoenix, and I am afraid again. But soon I see him for who he is. And I see Julian. At first I do not know if Julian is a boy or a girl, but then he talks and I can hear that he is a boy. I like his voice—it's deep and because he speaks slowly I can understand what he is saying, even though he has a strong French accent.

" 'ello, Taylor. Luke 'as told me about you."

"What has he said?" I ask.

"Good things," says Luke Phoenix. "Let's go inside and get something to eat."

We go inside and there is a big mess in the kitchen. My mother did not finish doing the dishes and then people have dirtied more.

"I'm babysitting tonight," says Luke Phoenix. "Martin's in bed asleep, and Julian and I were outside looking at the bats."

"Do you like bats?" I ask Julian.

"Oui, les chauves-souris," he says. "I am studying bats at the university. Or rather, I should say I'm at the university studying bats."

Luke Phoenix laughs and I don't know why.

"How were the aperitifs?" asks Luke Phoenix.

"They were only a kind of lemonade," I say. "But then we had dinner and it was stew. And birthday cake."

"Do you want any of these leftovers?" Luke Phoenix asks us. I shake my head, because that means no, but Julian holds out his hands and soon we are sitting in the living room, watching him eat the rest of a bowl of cold pasta.

"Are you sure you don't want that heated up?" asks Luke Phoenix, and Julian just laughs.

"In my family we eat a lot of leftovers because there are only three of us, my mother, my father, and me. I am so used to leftovers that I do not need food to be warm," he says.

Julian has thick dark eyebrows. I believe his nose would be called aquiline. He is wearing a white shirt with buttons down the front, and jeans. I think he looks hot in those jeans but I don't tell him that. I am sorry to hear that he is an only child.

After Julian finishes eating we play a game of cards. Then I decide to go to bed because of my personal care job in the morning.

I lie in bed and try to sleep but I can't. First I think about Julian being spoiled because he is an only child. Then I pick up an English-French translation book that I found on the bookshelf and read for a while. After that I go down to the kitchen and start to do the dishes. It is better to do them now than leave them until the morning.

There is a large wolf spider on the shelf behind the teapot. I carefully catch it in the tea strainer and put it on the ledge outside the open kitchen window. When the spider starts crawling along the ledge, I close the window. Since we have no screens it is best not to take a chance in case it wants back inside.

Luke Phoenix and Julian are in Luke Phoenix's bedroom, and after a few minutes they come out into the living room again and I can hear them talking. I know that they don't see me in the kitchen because they keep talking between themselves as if I am not here. Luke Phoenix's voice is sort of medium and Julian's voice is deep. I listen to them while I am running the water for the dishes.

"They asked her to babysit for the summer so she'd want to come to France with Penny," says Luke Phoenix. "It wasn't really fair and I said they should tell her the truth, but that's what happened. And now Dad and Penny are gone all the time, and I'm stuck here babysitting in the afternoons and evenings, which I wouldn't have been doing according to the original plan. The original plan was that I would cover the mornings when Dad was working and then he would take care of the rest."

"So you can't come to the wedding?" Julian asks.

"Probably not. I'll see. Maybe," says Luke Phoenix.

Julian says something in French and Luke Phoenix laughs; and then they go out onto the patio and I can't hear them anymore.

What did Luke Phoenix mean when he said that part about babysitting for the summer? Was that about me? Babysitting so I'd want to come to France with my mother?

Even though I am not asleep, I start feeling as if I am in a dream or a nightmare. How could I have come to France if I wasn't working for Alan Phoenix? Even if I had wanted to come, I would not have had the money. What did Luke Phoenix mean when he said that part about telling me the truth? This is like a nightmare, except I know that I will not wake up from it. It is stuck to me forever, this feeling of betrayal.

Finding out About the Lie

The water in the sink overflows and I have a mess to clean up, but my brain is short-circuiting with anger and I can't remember how to turn off the taps. The water runs and runs until there is water on the floor and everywhere and soap suds are sliding down the cupboard doors. I hear a car drive up to the house but I don't move. My mother and Alan Phoenix come into the kitchen. I am still standing at the counter, my jean dress soaked on the front, my feet in a slippery puddle that is getting larger all the time. I have sent anger from my core into the soles of my feet and now they are too heavy for walking. "Taylor, for God's sake, turn off the water!" my mother yells, running over to the sink.

"This is not a real job, is it?" I say, after she has turned off the taps. "This is not a real job and I am just here on a trick, and so I can't put it on my resumé, can I?"

My voice is in the red zone and climbing higher, and Alan Phoenix puts his hand on my arm and I fling myself away, slipping on the wet tiles. "Can I? This isn't something for my resumé—this is just something you made up so the both of you could spend the summer in France and I would want to come along!"

"Taylor, it isn't like that!" says my mother, calling after me because I am now in the living room and heading for the stairs. I feel like I am walking through mud except I am not.

"It isn't like that!" repeats my mother. "Come back and we'll talk about it! Your Grandma left us all this money and she would have been so happy to know we were traveling ..."

I slam my door and I do not care that it is hard on the hinges. I can hear voices downstairs and my mother's voice is in the red zone.

"What did you say to her?" she yells.

"Nothing! I didn't tell her anything, but somebody should have. Giving her this job wasn't fair and you know it!" says Luke Phoenix. "Everybody around here operates on lies and deception—nobody tells anyone how things really are!"

"Wait just a minute," says Alan Phoenix, and then I can't hear what they are saying. I open my door so that I can hear better, and then I hear Martin Phoenix's Tango voice: "What's the trouble? I'm trying to sleep."

"Sorry we woke you," says Alan Phoenix. "It's nothing."

"See!" shouts Luke Phoenix. "More lies!"

"What's up with you?" says Alan Phoenix. "This isn't about you."

"I have my own stuff going on," says Luke Phoenix. "I'm stuck here afternoons and evenings when you originally promised I'd just be with Martin for the mornings!"

"What stuff? What's going on that you can't spend an

evening or two with your brother?" says Alan Phoenix.

"Never mind!" says Luke Phoenix.

"She'd never have come all this way unless we promised her this job," says my mother, and now I'm running back down the stairs to where they are all standing in the living room.

"Lies and deception! You have ruined my resumé!" I tell her. "You have given me a summer with an empty resumé, and now I will never get a full-time job, and I will be stuck with you until you die and I am living alone!"

"Can't I have any fun?" my mother screams. "Can't I travel, just once, when the opportunity arises, without feeling guilty?"

I grab a cushion from the couch and throw it at the wall.

"Hold on, Taylor!" calls Alan Phoenix.

"Too late!" I yell. "I already let go!"

"Let's just all calm down and talk about this like normal people," says Alan Phoenix.

"Shut up!" I tell him. "We are normal people." I take a deep breath so that my voice does not stay in the red zone. "I want to be treated like an adult because I am nineteen and that means I am an adult. I am never late for work except once last summer when I was running away, and I am very responsible. I want to be told the facts about how things are and make my own decisions. You are NOT the boss of me!" I say to my mother. She starts to speak and then stops and tears come out of her eyes.

"I have to help you sometimes," she says finally. "I have to help you with things."

"No," I say. "I have to help myself. I will not be like

Stanley whose landlady did everything for him and fed him cornflakes even though he was afraid of them." They are quiet, looking at me.

"Who is Stanley?" says Martin Phoenix from his bedroom.

All the words about Stanley are in me waiting to come out. I know this is not the time for them, but I do not know what other words it is time for. I think of other things I could say, but this is not the time for them either, so I choke back what I am thinking: Gerbils are rodents. They can also be described as small mammals. They are nocturnal, and although they make good pets, they do make noise in their cages at night. They drum with their feet against the metal floor. This is their best way of communicating.

I look at Alan Phoenix and Luke Phoenix and my mother. They are standing in the living room and they are waiting for me to speak. Alan Phoenix has rubbed the back of his head so hard that all his hair is standing up on end. I take a deep breath. Then I take another. Then I feel lightheaded and stop breathing while I count to five.

"I am responsible for myself!" I say finally, thinking of Jean-Paul Sartre's little gray book. "That is how I am free. I am sometimes an unconscious subject of the world. I am sometimes a conscious object of the world. But I am also acting upon the world. I am going to Cassis again next Friday to see Adelaide and no one can stop me. And I am not babysitting Martin Phoenix any more unless it is a real job and it is called 'personal care assistant.'"

Luke Phoenix throws himself onto the couch and puts a pillow over his head. Alan Phoenix and my mother stay standing.

"It is a real job," says Alan Phoenix. "I'm—I'm sorry, Taylor, that you thought it was all a trick. Your mother and I did plan this so that you would want to come with us to France, but you have been a great babysitter—a great personal care assistant—and I hope, for Martin's sake, that you will continue."

"Who is paying me?" I ask.

My mother looks at Alan Phoenix.

"I am," he says. "Once your mother pays her share of the rent on this place, I can afford it."

"Rent?" my mother says. "Oh, yes. Yes, that's fine." Her forehead has that H of wrinkles in the middle of it.

The two of them look at me and I want them to put their eye gaze in another direction.

"Okay," I say. "I will not quit unless conditions worsen." I turn and go up the stairs, and then I stop.

"Good night," I say, wanting to end on a positive note. I think maybe my friend Luke Phoenix will take the pillow from his face and quote a poem, but he does not. Silence wells behind me as I walk up the stairs. Then I hear the Tango.

"Good night," Martin Phoenix calls from his bedroom. "At last sweet peace."

Friday, August 22

When I visit her today, Adelaide is still wearing her butterfly nightgown. Francine is wearing a blue and white pantsuit that is the color of my clock. After we eat supper, Adelaide pushes her plate away and asks if I'd like to see the garden.

"Mais, maman, tu es en chemise de nuit!" says Francine.

This time I know what Francine is saying: *But, Mother, you are wearing your nightgown!* Adelaide does not answer. She just gets up from the table.

"Okay," I say, and follow her.

We walk into the garden. I have already seen it but I don't mind seeing it a second time.

"When I was a girl my father made me an elephant out of potatoes," Adelaide says. She has told me this before. "He glued potatoes together and that was my Christmas present. And I treasured it. After it went rotten, we put it on top of the frozen garden and then I had the space back on my dresser."

We walk over to the stone bench.

"There are little fish in the pond," says Adelaide. "You will see them if we sit quietly for a minute." We settle on the stone bench and wait. Soon, bright orange shapes dart to the surface.

"The heron eats the big ones," she says.

"What?" I ask.

"Every so often, the heron comes and eats the bigger fish. Only the small ones escape him, but when they get big enough, they too are eaten."

"That's terrible," I say.

"It is what it is," she answers.

Rain begins to fall, making dimples on the surface of the water, and the orange shapes disappear.

"Swim, swim while you can," says Adelaide, "for tomorrow you may die."

"That's terrible," I say.

"It is what it is," she answers. She looks down at the water. "I like to get up in the middle of the night and play 'God Save the King' on the piano. It drives Francine crazy."

"God Save the King?" I ask.

"King George," she says. "A fine figure of a man. I took my students to see them both—King George VI and Queen Elizabeth—when they came to Canada in 1939. We went on the train, all the way to Regina. We stood on the corner of Victoria and Broad to view them as they drove by. My parents met us there—my father was driving the Essex 1928 at that time. When we got home, I had the children write down their favorite part of the trip. Most of them wrote about the royal couple, what they were wearing and all of that. One little fellow wrote: *My best part was when the train was going through the tunnel and even though it was daytime the air was black all over.*"

We go inside to her studio and the picture of clouds is still on the easel. I look at it carefully and the clouds seem quite safe.

"Try some more," she says, and I do. I take a long look out the window and then I use the charcoal to shade and soften, until the clouds seem to stick right out of the paper. Adelaide plays Liszt on the record player. She falls asleep on the couch on top of the patchwork quilt and I notice a large brown stain on the front of her nightgown. I think it might be gravy but I'm not sure.

After twenty-two minutes, Adelaide wakes up and pulls the patchwork quilt onto herself.

"I remember where each of these squares came from," she says.

"Oh," I answer. "You remember where each of the squares came from."

"You bet I do," she says. "Like this creamy silk. Annie Arbor brought this cloth, surprised us all because we thought she hadn't the means. Skinny as a rail, and all them kids. From England she was, answered an ad to marry Simon Howler. Lived in a tar paper shack they did, nothing much to eat in winter except molasses bread and what the neighbors brought. All the ladies sitting around, gossiping, sewing bits of their lives onto this quilt for my trousseau, and Annie Arbor steps in with that old burlap sack wrapped around her shoulders and carrying a stretch of creamy silk. Well, everyone was happy for her. It wasn't until later, after the quilt was done and colder weather hit, that we knew what happened."

"What happened?" I ask, shading in another cloud on the paper.

"It was her wedding dress," Adelaide said. "They found the rest of it all torn up. The day they found Annie hanging in the barn, dead as a doornail, poor dear soul."

"She killed herself?"

"Poor dear soul. It was her only way out."

I think of Stanley locked up in his room. How awful it would be to have only one way out.

"Do you remember all the women who made this quilt?" I ask.

"Every one of them. Martha Henry, who married the son of the richest man in town after being their servant for only six months. She was a mite stout on her wedding day, but no one thought any less of her. These scraps were left over from the dress she made her little daughter—pink tulle. Looked sweet on the child, that's for sure."

"And this blue one?" I go over to her and point to a dark floral print that repeats itself along the border.

"Well, this was one of my mother's. She had waited and waited for a store-bought Christmas dress, and when it finally came from the Eaton's catalogue, it was four sizes too big. She had to shorten it and take it in at the sides, and so there was lots of leftover material."

I think about my journal, and how each entry is like a piece of cloth that has been sewed into place on a quilt.

Adelaide gets up to examine the drawing on the easel. "Very good. You have been looking carefully," she says.

"Yes," I say. "I have been trying to see better."

"Being an artist takes more exercise than people think," she says. "To begin to draw is the first step. People these days have had enough of this crazy nonsense called contemporary art. In my day, three years of Art School meant architecture, perspective drawing, interior design, publicity, art history, the history of civilization, ceramics ... it took seventy different disciplines to make the diploma, and that shows in the work."

"You spent three years at Art School," I say.

"Did I meet you in Art School?" she asks.

"No." There is a silence. Luke Phoenix would fill it with a quotation, but I don't want to do that. "We met at the beach," I tell her.

"Oh," she says. After a minute she goes on. "There were thirty of us in the first year, twenty in the second, and only ten in the third. From these ten, only three got the diploma. I was one of those three."

"Did you go to Art School in Canada?" I ask.

"No," she says. "In Nice. I went to Art School there, at the Ecole Nationale d'Art Décoratif. My husband, the bastard, was trying to keep me happy after we moved to Europe, so he arranged for this. But then he left us."

"My father left my mother and me," I say.

"Was he a bastard, too?" she asks.

"I don't think so," I say. "They just wanted to be with different partners. He wants a woman named Sadie Richards who is tall and looks like Julia Roberts. She wants a man named Alan Phoenix who didn't actually hire me for the babysitting job this summer—but now he has. I don't know if he and my mother will get married, but if they do I will have two brothers. These two brothers could replace the brother who died before I was born and whose name did not get put on a gerbil. I hope I don't get Martin Phoenix as a brother before this summer is over because then I can't put *personal care assistant* on my resumé. I also hope that Harold Pinter and Samuel Beckett are not eating each other."

"Did we meet in Art School?" asks Adelaide. She is breathing heavily and I think she is trying to cough, but she does not.

"No," I tell her. "At the beach."

"When I was a girl my father made me an elephant out of potatoes," wheezes Adelaide. It's like her brain is stuck on this. "He glued potatoes together and that was my Christmas present. And I treasured it. After it went rotten, we put it on top of the frozen garden and then I had the space back on my dresser."

When I get back to the villa, Luke Phoenix and Julian are sitting at the dining room table with my mother and Alan Phoenix. Julian holds out a notebook.

"This is about a rare type of bats 'ere," he says. "I translated some things from French to English for you because of all of my materials being in French."

"Thank you," I say, taking the notebook. The title is *Bechstein's Bat*.

"Is Martin Phoenix asleep?" I ask.

My mother nods and that means yes.

"Julian and Luke are going to a wedding tomorrow," she asks. "Can you babysit?"

"No," I say. "But I am available as a personal care assistant if Alan Phoenix needs me."

"Taylor, why do you have to be so difficult?" she asks, but this is not a rational question and so I do not answer.

"Thank you," says Alan Phoenix. "Your mother has a class and I have to hang the paintings for the show. It opens on Sunday."

"Who is getting married?" I ask.

"Julian's ex-boyfriend," says Luke Phoenix.

"Oh," I say. There is a silence for one minute. "What class are you taking, Mom?"

She looks at me and doesn't answer for a moment.

"It's a cooking class," she says.

Friday, August 29

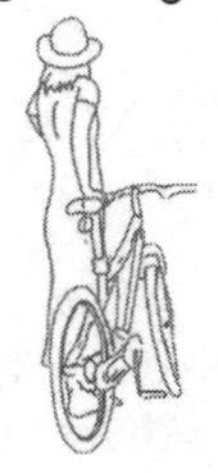

"I think Julian looked hot last weekend," Luke Phoenix says to me as I get ready to leave for Cassis on Friday. This is the third Friday that I have gone to visit Adelaide.

"He wasn't wearing jeans," I answer, and Luke Phoenix laughs.

"You can look hot in a suit," he says. "And Julian did."

"Well, maybe," I say. "But he's really not my type even though I like his deep voice. And he is spoiled."

"What?" asks Luke Phoenix.

"He told me he was an only child, and that means he is spoiled," I say. "I'm not sure how he is spoiled because it's probably not polite to ask."

"Spoiled?" Luke Phoenix repeats. "Where did you get that idea?"

"It's what happens when people have no siblings," I say. "My kindergarten teacher thought I was spoiled, but she didn't know about my dead brother. If she had known about Ashton she would not have told my mother that I was spoiled."

"Being spoiled means thinking only of yourself," says Luke Phoenix. "It can happen to anyone. Just because Julian's an only child, doesn't mean he's spoiled."

"Oh," I say. "Are you sure?"

"Yes," says Luke Phoenix. "Why—do you think Julian acts as if he thinks only of himself?"

I deliberate. "Well ... no," I say. "He translated that French text for me about bats. In that case he was thinking of me."

"Right," says Luke Phoenix. "There you go." I'm not sure what he means in that last part but I don't worry about it.

"Do you want to come to Cassis and meet my friend Adelaide?" I ask.

"No thanks, I'm babysitting," he answers. "But it's okay. Julian's going to hang out with us."

"It's called personal care," says Martin Phoenix with his Tango.

"Okay, yeah," says Luke Phoenix. "You're right, Martin."

"Martin's always right," says Martin Phoenix.

"Now that's going a little too far," says Luke Phoenix. "Let's thumb wrestle to see who's *always* right!"

I watch them thumb wrestling, their heads of red hair tilted over their game, and I think of how much I would like them to be my brothers. But not this summer. This is a summer for working, not a summer for my mother and Alan Phoenix to be getting married and me to acquire brothers.

"Julian's going to show you how to do some new experiments," says Luke Phoenix to Martin Phoenix. "He's going to be a scientist too, like you are, and he's got lots of ideas."

"Julian's going to be a biologist," I correct him. "Did you know that the only mammals naturally capable of real flight are bats? Did you know that the rare Bechstein's Bat roosts in woodpecker holes and particularly likes old trees, which is why this species favors our orchard?"

I watch Martin and Luke Phoenix thumb wrestle and then I listen to them talking and not once does Luke Phoenix quote from anything. It's like his brain was stuck on doing that, and now it's not. Now I think it's stuck on Julian—and I think that being stuck on Julian helps Luke Phoenix make more sense. Luke Phoenix likes and maybe loves Julian. If they fall all the way in love and get married, and Alan Phoenix and my mother get married, I will have three brothers: Luke Phoenix, Julian, and Martin Phoenix. If Martin Phoenix marries a girl, I could have a sister. I could end up in a big family after all and this would be okay with me. I actually like the idea of a big family. Just when I thought our small family was permanent, there are new opportunities on the horizon.

That means there are new opportunities coming our way, not anything about the actual horizon.

When I get to Adelaide's, her daughter opens the door. She is wearing a beige pantsuit with high heels and she is not wearing the blue and white dress or the blue and white pantsuit that reminded me of my clock. I can't remember her name but she stands in the doorway and doesn't say anything for a moment. Then she says, "Wait here." I wait for a long time. When she comes back, she has a large flat package that is wrapped in brown paper.

"Ceci est pour vous," she says, and then more slowly, "This is for you."

I take the package.

"Where is Adelaide?" I ask.

"I am sorry," says Adelaide's daughter. "Elle est morte il y a peu de temps. Je vais à l'hôpital en ce moment. A short while ago she is dead. Il fallait s'y attendre. It was to be expected. I am going now to the hospital." Her cheeks are wet. She starts to close the door and then she opens it wider and says, "Goodbye for now. I am—I am sorry." Then she closes the door.

I stand on the front step, holding the package. Adelaide was very old. It is common for very old people to die. Her daughter said that it was to be expected. But I did not expect it.

I walk around to the back yard and I sit on the stone bench, but the little orange fish do not dart to the surface. Maybe they got too big. Maybe the heron came. I see a few species of butterflies, all from the order Lepidoptera. This is the favorite food of the Bechstein's Bat. I look at my atomic watch. I sit for twenty-nine minutes. The little orange fish do not come. I go back to the bus stop and wait for the bus home.

I am used to gerbils dying. Walnut died first, then June, then Charlotte, then Hammy. Before that, my brother Ashton died, but I can't remember that because I wasn't born yet. Last spring, my grandmother died. I hope Harold Pinter and Samuel Beckett do not die but I am worried about them. When gerbils are stressed they can eat their own kind and there is a name for this, but I can't remember it right now.

When my grandmother died, she left my mother all her

money and that's why my mother could afford to buy a return airplane ticket to France. My grandmother left me a chess set but I gave it away because I don't like to play chess. I don't think Adelaide has left me money or a chess set. What she has left me is this package that I am holding in my arms and I do not know what is in it.

I wonder if she is wearing the butterfly nightgown now that she is dead in the hospital.

Cannibalism. That's what it's called when you eat your own kind.

I saw an online video once showing deer eating birds' eggs that were laid in nests on the ground. I never knew deer would do that. But they showed it in the video. These deer would walk around a field finding nests and then eating the birds' eggs out of them with their wide sharp teeth. I didn't think that could happen but then it was right there on the screen.

The Gift From Adelaide

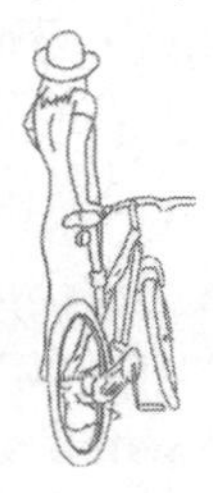

When I get back to the villa, I go upstairs and put the package on my bed. It is wrapped in brown paper and tied with string, and the string has knots in it. In order to open the package, I will have to either untie the knots or cut the string, and I'm guessing I will have to cut it because the knots look tight.

Stanley would probably not untie the package and he probably wouldn't cut the string. He would stand in front of the package and stay afraid of it until his landlady carried it away.

I go down to the kitchen to look for scissors, and when I find them I come back upstairs and take a deep breath. Then I cut the string. The paper does not fall away on its own. I have to unfold it from the corners and then pull it to the side, and while I am doing this it makes crackling noises that sound dangerous.

Inside the package I find a large canvas frame and lying against it is the picture of clouds that Adelaide and I drew. I remove the drawing and see that there is something painted on the canvas itself. I look at the painting. It is a painting of me. It is a painting of me with a bicycle. A white bicycle. I think it is done in acrylic wash, just like the paintings on Adeleide's livingroom walls. The colours look as if they are closed around so much light that the image seems to move as I look at it. I am not riding the bicycle. But I am not carrying it either. It looks as if perhaps I am in between riding and carrying, undecided.

I wonder what Adelaide meant about carrying her age. I wonder what she meant when she said that most people carry something. Did she know that I sometimes carry the white bicycle, like when I am in the woods and the trail makes riding too difficult? Did she guess that I carry other things as well, just as she carries her age—and that we all carry something?

All the answers to these questions are inside Adelaide but Adelaide is not here any more and so I cannot ask her. Adelaide is gone, taking everything inside of her. Where did Adelaide go? I ask myself this question over and over. I know that she is dead. But where did she go? This question repeats itself over and over in my brain until all the consonants disappear.

Missing Adelaide

On Saturday I ride the white bicycle to the market in Lourmarin. It is busy in the town square and I walk the bicycle through the crowds. There are colored scarves and tablecloths hanging at eye level. There are strings of pouches containing lavender. I see vendors selling shirts and blouses. I see stalls with meat—hams and chickens, and at the end, a lump of meat with the paper label *lapin* stuck onto it. I see big bowls of many different kinds of olives, and tables of melons and other fruits and vegetables. On one table there is a yellow bowl of candied lemons. I turn my head and sneeze.

I see an old woman in a butterfly dress. She is spooning olives into a plastic jar. I look at her carefully but it is not Adelaide. I feel wetness on my cheeks and I am crying. I pick up one of the T-shirts from a table and then put it down.

A vendor comes and points to me and says something in French. I think he is trying to steal my money but then I notice that the pouch I am wearing is unzipped and money is falling out of it. I quickly stuff the bills back inside and zip the pouch shut. The man smiles. I smile back and wave. This is just as smart as saying thank you.

There is nothing I want to buy at the market but I stay there as long as it is open. The thing I want to do, which is to see Adelaide, I cannot do. When the last stall closes, and the last bowl of olives is scraped into a bucket and put inside a white truck, I turn away from the town square and ride around the village. Eventually I ride up to the Lourmarin castle and lean the white bicycle against a wall, locking its wheels together so it can't be stolen. I pay my entrance fee and go through the gift shop, where there are lavender sachets twice the cost of the ones at the market. I climb the stairs to the highest turret. From here I can look down at the pond in the courtyard, where mottled koi rise among the water lilies. Last time I was here I saw a Gold Ogon koi that was probably worth a thousand dollars. I don't see it now. I wonder if the heron came for it, too. I see a Kohaku koi, and a Platinum koi, and two Ginrin koi, but no Gold Ogon.

I think about winter coming. Will the ponds freeze here like standing water freezes in Canada? I think about being here in the middle of a long winter, listening to the crackling ice. Deep in the pond the slow koi turn, the water congested with their milky breath. Heaviness fills me and I am afraid to take a step away from the railing but I am afraid to lean forward. Something flutters past and I remember spring, clover gathering the bees, their quick excited singing. I start walking away from the edge, towards the stairs. I think it was a Painted Lady butterfly back there but I am not sure.

If I look out past the castle grounds I can see the whole village. I can see where the market was, with all the wares for sale, but now it is gone. Now it is gone but it will come back next Saturday. It will come back but Adelaide will not. I look into the distance but I cannot see Cassis. I cannot see Adelaide's house, or the garden, or the pool where no little orange fish dart to the surface.

Supper With My Mother

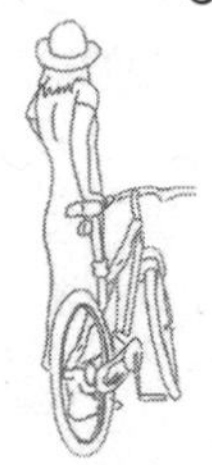

On Saturday night my mother has arranged for me to have dinner with her at the Auberge La Fenière, where she has been taking her cooking class every day for the past week. After biking home, I wipe spots out of my jean dress because my mother always notices things like that, and then Alan Phoenix gives me a ride to the hotel. He is mad because the rearview mirrors have both been ripped off the car and he wonders if the insurance will cover it.

"You should have flattened them when you parked," Martin Phoenix told him before we left the house, and that just made him madder.

Inside the restaurant, candles are on all the tables, and as soon as the waiter takes me to ours, I blow the candle out. Its flame is so yellow that I feel like sneezing, and then I do.

I sip my water and after six minutes my mother walks into the dining room and sits down opposite me at our table.

"You've already taken care of the candle," she says.

"No, I blew it out," I say.

"It might be a little dark to see our food," says my mother, looking around the room.

"What is the food?" I ask.

"It's a surprise," she says. "The first course is on its way. I hope you like it."

"So do I," I say, and my mother laughs.

A waitress brings out a tray with two plates, one for each of us.

"Foie gras de canard," she says. "Epicé et cuit au torchon, figues confites, pain aux noisettes et raisins."

I poke at the rolled circle of what looks like meat, bread, and dried fruit.

"Go ahead, try it," says my mother, putting a small forkful into her own mouth. "Mmm," she goes on. "It's really good!"

I try a small bite. It smells like butter and cinnamon. It tastes dusty and I don't eat any more of it.

"What is foie gras?" I ask.

"Fatty liver of duck," she says. "They force-feed the ducks so the liver gets bigger and extra flavorful."

"Force-feed?" I ask.

"With a tube, I think," says my mother. "But that's too much information. I'm sorry I told you that. Just forget about it, Taylor."

I feel sick to my stomach. I am glad I did not eat much of that stuff. They should not abuse animals this way.

"Well, you're going to like the rest of the meal. The main course is fish. You like fish, Taylor," she says.

"Turbot a la citronnelle cuit sur l'arête, avec lentilles au lard," says the waitress.

"Turbot—that's fish, right?" I ask my mother, translating the rest of the French myself. "Fish in a lemon sauce, with lentils and bacon."

She nods. I try some of the fish. It is good, but the lemony taste makes me sneeze. I scrape away the sauce and the bacon, and then try a lentil. Dusty. I only eat the fish.

We each drink a glass of fishy white wine called Château Fontvert White. My mother says it comes from an organic winery near Lourmarin. She tells me that the grapes are hand-picked and then the wine is fermented in French oak barrels for eight months.

"Can you taste the flowery aroma?" she asks.

"I just taste fish," I say.

"I taste a kind of a peachiness," she goes on. "I like the balance between roundness and acidity in this one."

I look at my glass. It is pear-shaped.

"I am sorry Adelaide died," says my mother.

"Why are you sorry?" I ask.

"I'm—I'm sorry for your loss," she says. I do not say anything for a few minutes.

"People can be friends even if they are not the same age," I say, finally. "You don't have to have a consistency of age in order to make a friendship."

My mother nods.

"Would you like to go to her funeral?" she asks.

"I don't know anything about that," I say, and suddenly I hate everything about this restaurant, I hate the meal, and most of all I hate my mother. I feel all the numbers and all the vowels and consonants in my head, yelling themselves into the red zone.

"We could phone her daughter and ask," she says.

"Ask what?" I whisper.

"Ask about the funeral," says my mother.

"But Adelaide won't be there, will she?" I say, my voice climbing into loudness. "And the rest of them are just strangers!"

"Shshsh," says my mother. "Taylor, think about where we are and let's just have dinner."

There is a long silence and eventually I fill it.

"Why don't we watch movies anymore?" I ask. My mother looks at me and the H of wrinkles is in the middle of her forehead.

"Movies?" she asks.

"We always used to watch movies but now we don't."

"I guess ... I guess we kind of forgot," says my mother.

I reach out my foot and kick over her flowered handbag.

"That's dumb," I say. "It's dumb to forget things."

My mother reaches over and touches my cheek and when her hand comes away, the fingers are wet.

"Taylor, I'm sorry Adelaide died," she says, for the second time.

"I know," I whisper. "You said it before."

"And I'm sorry we haven't been watching movies. I guess I just got busy."

"Why can't you be busy when you want to pester me, and *not* busy when we want to watch a movie?" I ask.

I try to think what I mean, and then I know. It's about the difference between children and adults, and it's about telling people the truth, but I can't find the exact words and the exact words are important.

My mother takes another sip of wine. "This wine is twenty dollars a bottle here but it is probably fifty in Canada. It goes well with fish, white meat with zesty sauces, goat cheese, and especially the foie gras."

The waitress comes to the table with more food on a tray.

"I do not want to eat any more, especially bloated duck," I say.

"Crème brûlée," says the waitress, putting down the dishes even though I asked for nothing. She also leaves a plate of cantaloupe slices. I try a piece. It is juicy and sweet and the best part of the meal.

"Do you want coffee?" asks my mother.

"I hate coffee," I say.

"The chef who was my teacher is very knowledgeable. She's earned this restaurant two Michelin stars," my mother continues.

"Oh," I say. "Did you cook all of our meal?"

"The whole thing," she answers. "Did you like it?"

"No," I say. "But I am sure you worked very hard because there was a lot of it."

I look at her and she doesn't say anything.

"I liked the melon," I say.

My mother has a look on her face that I cannot interpret.

"Are you thinking of something bad?" I ask.

"No," she says.

I look at her. She is. I'm sure she is. I wonder if she wants me to go to Adelaide's funeral. Then I wonder whether she wanted me to like the food she made. I look at the table. It is so perplexing to try and figure people out. But even if people cannot speak the same language, they can learn to understand each other.

"We have to tell each other the truth," I say.

My mother puts down her wine glass.

"We do," she says. I look at her. "Well ..." she continues. "Most of the time we do. But sometimes ..." Her voice stops.

"Sometimes and all the time we should tell each other the truth," I say. "Adelaide and her daughter lived together and Francine wanted to be the boss of Adelaide, but Adelaide wouldn't let that happen. And nobody can be bossed without their own compliance."

"I'm sorry Adelaide died," says my mother for the third time.

"She kept on making choices," I tell her. "She played 'God Save the King' on the piano in the middle of the night because she wanted to. I am going to do that."

"You're—you're going to learn to play the piano?" says my mother.

"No, I mean I am going to make my own choices. From now on, I am an adult and I will be making the choices about myself. That is something I have control over. You have control over yourself and you should just think of the choices you have to make. If I am going to be independent, we both have to keep on choosing for ourselves and not the other person."

I can't tell if her eyes are wet or not. I think they are.

"I don't know ... it's hard," she says. "You don't always understand things, and—"

"*Nobody* understands everything, Mom," I say. "Nobody could possibly understand everything. You certainly don't."

"Well, I ..." she says, and her voice trails off and she makes kind of a choking sound. “It’s hard, Taylor. You have no idea how hard it is for me. When you’re like this, when you’re sad or mad, I want to comfort you and give you a hug, but that doesn’t work with you. Whatever I do doesn’t work. It’s always been that way. When you were little, people thought it was my fault, and that you were spoiled—”

“People who are spoiled think only of themselves,” I interrupt. “Maybe I used to be like that but then I started learning about other people’s perspectives.” She nods.

“Nobody understands everything,” I repeat as a placeholder, but then I can’t think of what to say next. We sit in silence. Finally, I say, “I do know how to ask questions. I can use all the five w’s. That’s something. That’s something I bet Stanley couldn’t do.”

Something about my mother’s mouth changes. Is she smiling?

“Yes, asking questions is something,” she says.

“Stanley *couldn’t* ask any questions and that’s why he didn’t have any way out of his bedroom where his landlady bossed him all the time. Well, he might have had one way out, but that’s the way out Annie Arbor used and it’s a bad way.”

“Annie Arbor?” asks my mother, but I do not respond. There is no use telling her Adelaide’s stories. Those stories were between me and Adelaide and I am going to keep them for myself.

I feel as if a great weight is lifting off me. I look at my mother sitting on the other side of the table and I am not afraid anymore about my future, whatever it may be, because I am not—I repeat *not*—going to be like Stanley.

"I am not like Stanley," I tell her, just so she understands completely what I am talking about.

"I know," she says. "You are much more independent than Stanley, from what you have said about that play."

"You think I am independent?" I ask.

She nods.

"I know I am independent," I say. "I can use strategies when I am sad or mad, and Stanley could not. He didn't know about postponing difficult topics until a better time, or deep breathing, and he kept all his anger in his core. I am not like Stanley and I am not waiting any longer, either," I say, thinking about that other play, Beckett's play *Waiting for Godot*. "All this time when I thought I was waiting for no one, I was really waiting for you, Mom."

"Taylor, what are you talking about?" she says.

"There's something I have been waiting for in order to be an adult. It's not having a boyfriend. It's not taking classes at university. It's not getting a job. I have done all those things and I am going to keep doing them. But they do not make me an adult. I'm not waiting any longer, Mom. Because I know what I am waiting for. I am waiting for you."

"But I can't ..." she says, "... I don't know—"

"I'm waiting for you to let me be free," I tell her.

My mother stares at me and then she looks down at the table. Then she looks at me again.

"I should be free, Mom. I should be."

She keeps looking at me and it is uncomfortable because I do not want to look back and so I look at her eyebrows.

"I am not just someone acted on by the world—I am acting on it," I tell her. "I am more than just a daughter and a sister. I am more than just a woman with a white bicycle. I am someone who can save an old lady from the sea, who can take care of a boy I am assisting, who can read the words of people like Jean-Paul Sartre and think about freedom."

She nods but I am not sure she gets it and so I go on.

"I am a student and a friend. I might be a biologist some day. I might be an artist. I might be a writer. But whatever I do, Mom, I am free to choose. I need to be free to choose."

I see her nod again and then she brushes her eyes.

"I get it," she says.

"You get the picture," I say, just to be sure.

"Yes," she answers, and kind of laughs. I'm not sure why.

"It's hard when things change," she says, and wipes her eyes again. "It's hard on me. Just when I think I'm getting good at ... at how things are, they change."

"Join the club," I say. Then I look at her to make sure she's understood. "I'm not talking about a real club," I tell her.

"I know," she says, and kind of gulps.

"Sometimes I might need an island of stability," I say, remembering how I felt in the hotel room when I was worrying about our lost luggage. "But not all the time. Nobody needs an island of stability all the time, Mom."

"Okay," she says. "I ... I understand that, Taylor. I do."

"It takes two of us," I remind her, just so this is very clear. "Stanley could have tried to be more independent but probably Meg wouldn't let him. You have to let me be an adult—just like when you are old, I will let you be an adult."

"What?" she asks.

"When you are old, you might come and live with me, like Adelaide and Francine. At first I thought it would be excellent to be the boss of you, but then I decided that it would be awful because you are too stubborn. So I won't try to be the boss of you after all if you are living with me, like Adelaide lived with Francine."

She laughs but when she looks at me I see that her eyes are wet. I think she is probably sad about her cooking.

"But we can watch movies sometimes," I say, just to make sure she hasn't forgotten about this.

"Okay," she says, wiping at her cheeks with the napkin. "Okay, Taylor."

"I am glad you took this cooking class from the chef with the Michelin stars," I tell her. "Even though I did not like the food, someone will probably like it. You could open your own restaurant in Saskatoon. You would be good at that. Except do not force-feed the ducks. Force-feeding the ducks," I tell her, "is mean."

"I promise," she says softly and I am very relieved until she says, "I promise I ... I will try to let you go, Taylor. I'm not saying I can do it soon or even very well, but I will try."

"Okay," I say, glad to hear that, but sorry about the ducks because it appears that I still have some work to do about the foie gras.

"Maybe it just takes practice," I say.

"What?" she asks.

"Letting me be an adult. Maybe we both just have to practice," I say.

Going Home

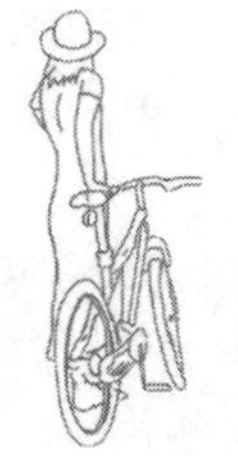

Today is the day that we go back to Canada and our summer in France will be over. My mother got up very early to pack. I can hear her banging around in the kitchen and I am not sure what she is thinking. She could be chasing spiders. She could be washing somebody's breakfast dishes. She could be cooking, although this is unlikely since we are soon going to be leaving the villa. I am not sure what she is thinking but her thoughts are up to her.

Last night, I dreamed I was riding the white bicycle through the vineyard at the bottom of the hill near Lourmarin. The path was a bit rough, like that playground when I was little and biking for the first time without training wheels, but I am now an experienced rider and I stayed in the seat. I could see the grapes forming round and ripe on the vines. I could smell the lavender in the neighboring fields. I came to the woods and I began to carry the white bicycle, remembering that after I carried it for a while, soon I would be able to ride again. I listened very carefully but I couldn't hear my mother calling. All I could hear was my own breath.

Life is like that. Sometimes things are heavy in your arms, and at other times, you are lifted forward to places you would not have discovered without the burden you have carried.

Looking backward, I can see bicycle tracks in the sandy soil but if I look ahead all I see is the distance, blue as the Luberon mountains, inviting as the cool breeze that pushes up through the hot air. It is a distance I can navigate, a space that I will be moving through with the wind in my hair. And there is no precipice ahead of me, just good solid land. There is nothing to worry about, not really.

Acknowledgments

Taylor's existential ideas in this volume have been inspired by Jean-Paul Sartre's "little gray book": *The Wisdom of Jean-Paul Sartre* (New York: Philosophical Library), which includes selections from his best-known work, *Being and Nothingness.*

Richard Ellenson invented the Tango speech device in 2006, after this book is set, and apologies for sending the invention back into the early 2000s in this story.

Gratitude to the Canada Council for the Arts, for supporting the development of this book.

Many thanks to Taylor Crowe for his brilliant cover art and for his inspirational work on the subject of autism (see http://www.taylorcrowe.com).

Appreciation to Dr. Tina Arora who served as a consultant on the authenticity of Taylor's perseverations, special thanks to Dr. Culley Carson-Grefe for her timely and accurate advice on the French language, and gratitude to Padmaja

Sarathy along with the Association for Childhood Education International Special Interest Forum for their ongoing work and inspiration.

For all their love and support, thanks to Sandra and Paul Beckett, Liliane Marco, and my family and friends. Special thanks to Connor for his savvy proofreading, and to Dwayne for his steadfast encouragement and ready ear.

Thanks to Richard Dionne, Cheryl Chen, and the rest of the team at Red Deer for their solid support. To my editor Peter Carver: heartfelt thanks for being such a tremendous co-walker in this sustained journey we have had together with Taylor Jane.

Interview with Beverley Brenna

This is the third novel to explore the life of Taylor Jane Simon. What is it about this character and her life that has prompted this series of stories?

As a writer, I want to fill in gaps where available literature seems to be missing something or someone. This way I think I can make a difference to readers. When I first wrote about Taylor in *Wild Orchid,* I wanted to tell a story from the perspective of someone whose voice I hadn't heard published before: the voice of a young woman with Asperger's Syndrome.

In the first novel of the series, I think Taylor presents a fairly universal growing-up picture of a girl hoping for a boyfriend. I recognized that at the end of *Wild Orchid,* her journey toward adult independence wasn't finished, and so I wrote the next book in the series, *Waiting for No One*. In that story, Taylor strives to explore post secondary education and the world of work, in order to continue her journey towards maturity.

In *The White Bicycle,* the final book in the series, I wanted Taylor to look inward instead of outward as part of her growing-up journey, and I see her here as taking a giant step into adulthood.

When I started, I didn't intend to write three books about Taylor—I thought I'd be lucky to finish just one! I'm glad Taylor was able to sustain her story through three books. This gave me the opportunity to get to know her deeply, and to learn more about Asperger's Syndrome.

As she reaches out for independence, Taylor displays a capacity to look back as well as to dream of what her life could be like in the future. This strikes me as an unusual aspect of the story, since most young people of her age don't spend a lot of time contemplating their past. Do you think Asperger's Syndrome prompts this sort of self-awareness, or is it specific to Taylor?

I think Taylor has learned to be particularly reflective due to her struggle with social communication. She doesn't make predictions very easily and she uses information from past experiences to navigate through present situations as best she can. The more experiences she has, the better she can chart her course, and so the older she gets, the more she is able to search for a past pattern on which to act. Essentially,

Taylor combs through her past looking for information that will help her understand the present.

For example, she has learned how to use "social scripts" to have conversations. She knows from experience that if she repeats part of what a person says to her in conversation, she can keep the conversation going. People who don't have Asperger's Syndrome might do this automatically, without thinking about it, but Taylor needs to concentrate on learned strategies because conversations aren't easy for her. I think of Taylor as a kind of historian, and the history she most needs to concentrate on is her own!

This story has a strong sense of place. You yourself have been to the Lourmarin area. Was that why you decided to send Taylor there? What appealed to you about Taylor's finding the impetus for her declaration of independence somewhere far from her home?

When I was thinking about continuing Taylor's life story, I knew that I wanted her to experience a sustained period of long-distance travel—because I have noticed that characters in books who are "differently abled," like Taylor, rarely travel. Taylor travels a few hundred kilometers in *Wild Orchid*, and ventures even further in *Waiting for No One*. But I wanted to close her story with a truly international travel experience. This is an example of what other published books seem to be missing and I hope my writing will fill the gap.

For this final coming-of-age instalment, I also wanted to include the theme of existential philosophy—basically, ideas about the meaning of life. So I looked to the writing of Jean-Paul Sartre, one of the founders of existentialism, to help me think about this. I knew that Jean-Paul Sartre was born in Paris, so at first I thought Taylor might go to Paris. Then I looked into the placement of French art schools, and since I found a great number of them in the south of France I decided that the landscape of the Lourmarin area might work to frame the story.

I'm especially glad I chose the south of France because my husband and I spent some time there on our honeymoon twenty-five years ago. Writing this book allowed me to revisit those happy times! All that wonderful food! I gained ten pounds in two weeks. My most favorite meals involved duck roasted in honey and garlic, and crème brulee—a rich combination of cream and sugar with a burnt sugar topping. And I adored the chocolate-filled croissants, just as the characters in the story do.

Taylor has an intense, though brief, relationship with Adelaide—a vivid and compelling character. It almost feels as if she is drawn from a person you have known—is that true?

While writing *The White Bicycle,* I thought a lot about my mother as I developed the character of Adelaide. At 95 years old, my mom had managed to hold onto a sense of meaning and importance that I think is often lost when people enter their senior years. Although Adelaide does not at all encapsulate my mother as a person, several of my mother's experiences—the story about the potato elephant, for example, and the visit to Regina to meet King George VI—have been adapted into Adelaide's repertoire. In addition, Adelaide has my mother's sense of *joie de vivre*—the joy of life—which Mom demonstrated until the day she died.

My mother was also an incredible storyteller, and I think that much of my writing contains brief anecdotes that are shaped by the way my mom might have collected them—just because she loved meeting new people and drawing out details about their lives.

As with the first two books, this story is told in the first person. This allows the reader to gain insight into Taylor's thought processes. There is a distinctive rhythm to the narrative. How did you arrive at the voice we hear in the story?

In my work with people who have Asperger's Syndrome, I have noticed many differences in their prosody: pitch, loudness, tempo, and rhythm. I have a background in theater, so I'm pretty good at picking up on speech patterns and copying them—although you can ask my university students about my laughable fake French accent! In addition to my attempts to copy speech patterns from real life, I think some forms of theater seem to reproduce the speech patterns of people with autism, and this has been a resource for me. The plays of Harold Pinter and Samuel Beckett, for example, contain characters who speak with similar differences in prosody. I've never heard anyone else talk about this, but to my ear, some of the characters in Pinter's and Beckett's work appear to see the world through an autistic perspective as well as use what I think are recognizably unique language patterns. Both Pinter's *The Birthday Party* and Beckett's *Waiting for Godot* are plays mentioned by Taylor in my books, and she even names her gerbils after these famous writers. Quite possibly the re-reading of dialogue within these plays gave me a stronger ear for Taylor's voice and perspective than I might otherwise have had.

Some people might think of Asperger's as an illness, but you obviously see it as a way of life, with its own richness as well as its challenges.

I like how Dr. Tony Attwood, a clinical psychologist (see http://www.tonyattwood.com.au) confirms what I have noticed in the students with whom I've worked—that having Asperger's means seeing the world in a different way, not in a defective way. He particularly emphasizes the fact that having Asperger's brings gifts as well as challenges. It seems to me that in our world today, we need creative thinking to solve all kinds of problems—thinking that's different from the kind that created those problems in the first place. Perhaps different types of brains can help in this regard. I hope so!

One thing about people with Asperger's is that they often have amazing visual memories. Taylor certainly does, and this helps her in many aspects of her life—as a biology student, a tourist, and an artist.

We are fortunate to have an original painting by Taylor Crowe for the cover of *The White Bicycle*. Could you tell us how this came about?

I met Taylor Crowe in Miami in January 2012. I was there to attend the awards ceremony at a conference sponsored by the Council for Exceptional Children's Division on Autism and Developmental Disabilities, where I was honored as the first Canadian recipient of a Dolly Gray Children's Literature Award—that was for *Waiting for No One*. I was totally pumped. Who wouldn't want a trip to Miami in January, when the temperature in Saskatchewan was -40°C?

Taylor Crowe was one of the keynote speakers at the conference, and I was tremendously impressed by his speech about his own personal journey with autism. I was also struck by his work as a visual artist—he's a graduate of the California Institute of the Arts. I suddenly knew he would do a fabulous job of designing the cover of my next book. Luckily my publisher at Red Deer Press agreed! For more about this brilliant young man and his art, check out http://taylorcrowe.com.

Thank you, Bev.

About the cover artist

Taylor Crowe is an artist and lecturer on topics related to autism. He is a graduate of The California Institute of the Arts, where he majored in Character Animation.

Taylor was diagnosed with autism after undergoing extreme behavioral changes and losing almost all of his language skills by age three.

Years of therapy, along with the persistent involvement of family, friends and other individuals in and outside the school environment ultimately provided Taylor the communication skills and social skills he needed to successfully interact with others.

Once discovered, his artistic capabilities and gifts were nurtured, not only as a source of enjoyment and fulfillment for Taylor, but as a strategy to further enhance his social capabilities.

Taylor's lectures cover topics such as his recommendations to teachers, therapists and families of individuals with autism as well as techniques for developing positive and meaningful relationships with neurotypical peers. Taylor also gives presentations on topics related to art, animation and giftedness in autism.

His art is in collections throughout North America.

Taylor lives in Cape Girardeau, Missouri.

To learn more go to: www.taylorcrowe.com